A Broken River Books original

Broken River Books
10660 SW Murdock St
#PF02
Tigard, OR 97224

ISBN: 978-1-940885-38-4

Printed in the USA.

HEATHENISH

A NOVEL

BY

KELBY LOSACK

BROKEN RIVER BOOKS

PORTLAND, OR

for Erika

"Step into the shadows, we can talk addiction."

—Earl Sweatshirt, "Grief"

RED LIGHT

I warn Kim before we get in the car that this isn't going to be a fun ride, and that I've been drinking.

She holds her hand out for the keys.

Houston shrinks in the rearview. A pink sky enveloped in swirling black clouds.

Kim says, "So?"

I watch the highway roll by in a yellow street lamp-lit blur beneath us. "This isn't working for me," I say.

"What, how when we come down to visit, you stay with your parents instead of with me and the kids?"

"Don't drag the kids into this."

"I'm not dragging them anywhere, they're right there." She tilts her head to the backseat.

Destiny says "da-da" over and over and shakes her rattle in a maestro-conducting-an-orchestra type of way. Anjelica snores softly. Deandre kicks my seat and giggles. I tickle his

1

feet and say, "You better stop that," and he kicks harder and faster and giggles louder.

Three kids three years three houses together three friends' couches alone three years a hundred thousand miles three years how many pills three years how many fist-sized holes in the drywall three years two security deposits we never got back how many times cheated on three years zero fucks given three years I can't take anymore three years enough.

Kim's breathing shakes. She says, "What is it you want?" Death grip on the wheel, fingers becoming embedded in the leather; probably why she doesn't bother to wipe the tears rolling silent down her face.

I dig deep to find some sort of sympathy or compassion or whatever it is when you're trying to tell your wife you want to leave her manipulative, lazy, cheating bitch ass, but don't want to be a dick about it.

I come up empty. Just say it. "I want to stop pretending. I don't love you. I don't think I ever did. I think I was a stupid, impulsive teenager and, yeah, I definitely never loved you."

She says, "Stop," then after a minute: "I loved you."

I say, "No, you didn't."

She says, "How do you know?"

I say, "I think I would have noticed."

Deandre shouts, "Red means stop!"

Kim slams on the brakes just over the white line. We wait without words for the light to turn green. It seems to take forever. I contemplate how this could be a metaphor for our entire relationship. That's probably the pills thinking for me again.

Not long after we moved to Victoria, into the house Kim's aunt owns but doesn't live in, a friend and I were walking around the neighborhood and found a pit bull chained to a tree in a dirt yard. The chain stopped a few inches out of reach of a stagnant water bowl. I told my friend we should steal that pit bull, and that's what we did. I named him Tupac.

Tupac jumps up and down behind the fence when we pull into the driveway. The headlights cast shadows of his ears flopping and his tail wagging and when I scratch his head and squeeze his neck, I swear he smiles. As if it needs to be said, I say it anyways: "He's going with me."

I put the kids in bed and turn my back on the open master bedroom and fall asleep watching Netflix on the couch and the next day, we break the house down into boxes divided and marked with our names.

Kim's parents pay for a lawyer whose office chair is a yoga ball and we go together to sign the papers.

Kim's mother, aunt, and grandmother manage to back a U-Haul in the driveway but prove worthless loading it up. I help carry the bed, the dresser, the 72-inch tax return-purchased television, the crib, and the toddler beds into the trailer. I tell Kim's mother to just give up on trying to figure out the car seats and I secure them in the minivan. I buckle the kids in and kiss their heads and say, "I'll see you later," and they all smile and even though I tried explaining divorce to them on a toddler level, I'm not sure they quite get it yet.

I ask Kim's aunt where she wants me to leave my copy of the house key when I leave and she says to just leave it on the kitchen counter and she gives me a hug and I stand stiff with shock, my arms at my sides. She hugs me long enough for Kim to raise an eyebrow and Kim's mother to sneer and doesn't let go until I tap out on her back.

She says, "Take care of yourself. You're a good man."

I say, "Okay."

They leave and I push all of my boxes against a wall in the living room and open the front and side doors and throw a ball down the hall, out into the yard, and Tupac runs in and out of the house while I wait on my dad and my little brother Brandon and my sister's fiancé Mitch to come help me move back to the area code I thought I had left behind for good.

"I wish we had a place of our own," my dad says. "One with a fence. There's nothing we can do, though. Even if the landlord allowed it, I don't want a dog that size in the house."

I swallow an anchor. "I understand."

4

"I mean, I love Tupac. He's a great dog. I wish there was something we could do."

"I know," I say. "I get it."

It's midnight when we stop at the shelter. My dad drives around back to the afterhours drop-off kennels. He lets the tailgate down and Tupac jumps out and spins circles. He rears up and puts his front paws on my chest and we slow dance to no music one last time.

My dad drops off the bag of dog food and fills out the form and slides it in the mail slot in the door.

Tupac follows me into an empty kennel and I sit on the ground and he lays across my lap, unaware he's at least thirty pounds past lap dog size. His tail slaps the chain link walls. He's oblivious as an infant on a doorstep. I squeeze his neck and touch my head to his and cry and at some point, I get up, tell him "stay," and I lock the kennel and leave without actually saying goodbye.

We fill my parents' shed with boxes. Brandon and I carry the few going in the bedroom in one trip. The beds are made.

Brandon says, "I figured you'd want bottom bunk."

I say, "Yeah, that's fine."

He says, "Did you put in for your transfer?"

"I get my schedule tomorrow." I face plant on the bed with my clothes on.

The bed frame creaks. Brandon's jeans fall from the top bunk to the floor.

He hangs his head over the edge of the bunk, says, "Want to watch a movie?"

I say, "Sure."

I close my eyes and the nightmares begin before I see which movie he picks.

When I approach the entertainment store to get my schedule, Vyron is there on the patio with the latte drinkers and menthol smokers, pacing in a three-piece suit, heading up an animated conversation.

I say, "You asking to get robbed in that suit, motherfucker."

Vyron spins on his heels, shoulders arched/chin out, ready to talk shit and hit somebody. He sees the shit-talking motherfucker is me and shouts, "Baby boy!" Throws his arms around me. "Oh, man," he says, back to pacing, "what the fuck. How long you down for?"

"A good minute. I just transferred here." I point to the store moniker. "Going to get my schedule now to see when I start."

His smile turns devilish. He snatches a cigarette from unsuspecting lips and takes a drag, gives it back. He says, "So you're back, huh?"

I say, "Yep."

He nods. "I fucking run this city now, you know."

"Is that so?"

"Yuh. They're going to build a fucking statue of me." He poses like a statue, hands on his hips/chest out/skyward gaze.

We laugh.

He says, "I can't believe you're back, man. I work at that dealership right there." He points across the parking lot to the very next building off the highway. "I sell cars and collect people's credit like a true thug." He shakes his head and grins. "We're going to get into some hoodrat shit."

"Fuck yeah," I say. "Just like old times."

"No," Vyron says. "Just like new times."

That night, I park my car at Vyron's new place on Sixth Ave and slide in the shotgun of his Altima. We cop a bottle of electric blue bum wine and go booze cruising through an aristocratic neighborhood. Chopped and screwed trap music distorts the speakers. We pass the bottle back and forth and catch up on each other's lives. We look at all the pretty houses with the front porch chandeliers and iron gate fences. We swerve; almost hit a speed limit sign. We dip in and crawl back out of a ditch.

Vyron hands me the bottle, quarter to empty, says, "Kill it before we hit this light."

I aim the bottom of the bottle at the ceiling and dome the wine and Vyron speeds up and runs through the light as it turns red. Tires screech and a car horn blasts. I toss the empty bottle out the window and hear the shattering of glass against cement.

Cars are parked everywhere back at Vyron's place—in the driveway and parallel in the street.

"Jesus," I say. "How many people live here?"

Vyron says, "Enough to start a fucking cult," which turns out to be four roommates, a landlord who lives in the master suite, and a golden Labrador who very much resembles the cartoon lioness she's named after.

Nala sleeps on the floor in the first bedroom, getting secondhand high with Eric and his boyfriend Anthony. They're harmless stoners, the three of them.

Stephen is a motor head. The gutted Ranger on cinder blocks in the backyard is one of his projects.

Earl owns dozens of stringed instruments and is mediocre at best on all of them, but that's okay, because he's punk rock and doesn't give a shit.

The landlord, whose name escapes me, is a twelve-year-old looking motherfucker who stole Satan's goatee. That's how Vyron introduced him to me. It's a fitting description. He's also a soft-spoken, straight edge vegan who says shit like *holy moly* and *that's groovy*.

The first week of being back in my hometown, Vyron and I turn the Sixth Ave house into a civic center for hoodrats. When the moon comes out, we fulfill our vices. It's like heaven, if heaven had a secret back room with a filthy mattress beneath a broken Bowflex.

TRAIN

We walk on train tracks, the black dot on the horizon beginning to take shape. Vyron breathes a cloud over his chapped lips into his chapped hands. I show him the orange bottle with the Rx symbol and my name on the label.

He says, "Holy fuck, you got Addies."

I say, "I'm severely ADD. That's the doctor's diagnosis. Told him I can't focus on anything for shit, can't sit still, and my mind keeps me up at night. He gave me a test and I'm in the highest percentile of severity in adult ADD. Heard you were, too."

The train looks like a train now. We keep walking towards it.

Vyron grins when I tip a tablet out into his hand. He says, "You tried it yet?"

"Every possible way almost."

"You sniffed it?"

"Nah. I'm scared of buckshot nose."

Vyron dry swallows the tablet. Makes a bitter face. "It'd

taste better up your nose," he says. "There's this old dude I work with—like, seventy-something—he's into all kinds of hard shit. Selling and using. He doesn't look it so much, though. He just looks old." Vyron blinks and it hits him. His head rocks back and he smiles and spins in circles, karate chopping the air. "I feel like a fucking superhero, man," he says. "Like I could probably jump over this train. Or run right through the middle of it."

He zones in on the engine screaming at our faces and I push him off the tracks one way and jump off the other side and clench my eyes against the wind.

HOODRAT CHRISTMAS

The house on Sixth Ave is alive tonight. I rub shoulders with strangers, share breathing space with unfamiliar faces. Vyron plugs his laptop into a loudspeaker and plays a beat he made and we get a freestyle circle going. Beads of sweat fly from the swinging hair of intoxicated dancers. Liquor-touched tongues twist together. A golden waterfall is tipped over a tabletop. Someone throws a fist and we throw him out and go back to getting throwed.

Double-stacked Styrofoam cups full of purple stuff.

Open baggies across the floor like popcorn at the cinema.

One hundred hands, five hundred lighters.

Beer cans accordioned on the lawn.

Vomit and piss and someone passed out on the lawn.

I sniff some devil dust and sip some lean and everything is sideways.

It's Christmastime, and like good Americans, we try to fabricate euphoria and pretend for a moment we have something to celebrate.

* * *

Trenton, an old friend I haven't seen since prom, walks in the front door. I wave him down from across the room and his face lights up. He shoves his way over and picks me up in a bear hug. He says, "It's been forever." He sets me down and points to the guy shadowing him. "This is Rafael. He's got some dust in the attic, but he's a trill motherfucker."

I say, "What's up."

Rafael smiles, hangs his head. Hands in oversized jacket pockets.

Trenton says, "You'll never believe what just happened," and he opens a baggy with a paisley-shaped/palm-sized cluster of dro that smells like pineapple. We smoke the shit in Eric and Anthony's room out of a bong and Trenton tells the story of how he and Rafael copped the pot from a fat old man at a gas station who traded them a full gift bag for two Walmart cards they'd gotten from their grandmothers for Christmas.

Eric says, "Sounds like Santa came early."

Rafael giggles. Smoke billows from his mouth to the ceiling and he says, "He sees you when you're sleeping."

Vyron and I stumble out to the back porch, where Javi tokes a spliff and plays guitar and Ricardo sings in his best Tom Waits voice about falling out a window with confetti in his hair.

"These motherfuckers think they live on my porch," Vyron says.

Rafael is slamming his fist on the table and ranting to a red-from-laughter Trenton about how Jesus was conceived when Mary had tentacle sex with Satan.

Ricardo says at the end of a verse while Javi continues playing, "I thought god knocked up Mary."

Rafael says, "Goddamnit," strikes his palm on the table like a tent revival preacher. "God is asexual. He doesn't even have junk. That's why the whole Old Testament, he slays anyone who breaks his rules on who or when they can fuck, 'cause he's pissed he can't get any."

Trenton falls out of his chair.

Ricardo says he doesn't believe in god.

Javi says, "How can you not? I mean, look at the stars."

We all look up. The constellations shine bright against the black sky.

"Yeah, I believe in stars," Ricardo says. "I can see those." He taps me with the back of his spliff hand, passing it, and asks what I believe in.

I take a long drag and some of the paper comes off on my tongue and I spit it out. "I believe in stars, too." I shrug. "And myself, I guess." I try passing the spliff back and he shakes his head and points his chin at Vyron, so I pass to Vyron, and the circle begins.

"Facts, not faith," Ricardo says. "That's me, basically."

"Yeah." I cough smoke until my eyes water. I pick up a

40 off the table, but all that's left is witch piss. I can feel my face turning red. Vyron hands me a plastic cup full of lean and I knock it back. Clear my throat, wipe my eyes. Ricardo stares at me, waiting for a more insightful response. I say, "I can't believe in something I don't know. I was raised in church, but I've never met a god."

"Same here. If one exists, he's abandoned us. So fuck him, right?" Ricardo smiles and tells Javi to play a different song, another Tom Waits tune, and he sings again in a gravelly baritone.

The spliff makes it to Trenton. He says, "Why does god have to be a man?" He blows a smoke ring, swirls his finger around inside it, and puts the spliff in Javi's mouth while he strums.

I shrug again. "I'm indifferent if she or he does exist. It's just like people—I don't fuck with you if you don't fuck with me. If there's a god, when I die, that's what I'll tell her: 'I'm not angry or jealous or anything that you never bothered with me. I made it my whole life without you, though, so nothing personal. It's just simply I don't fuck with you.' Then I'll turn around and walk the other way."

In the early AM hours, people with unfamiliar faces become people with names. Seth—an old friend of mine from back in the *hey, let's start but never go anywhere with several shitty punk bands* days—dribbles whiskey and slurs introducing me to a pink-mohawked woman named Syd, then all six feet and two hundred-plus pounds of him passes out on the floor. It's just the three of us in Earl's room, shut off from the party. Seth and I were jamming on Earl's guitars and catching up when Syd walked in and sat against the wall to listen. Now she gets up and steps over drunk Seth to sit on the bed next to me. It's not awkward how close she sits, this woman whose name I learned ten seconds ago, because I've washed down a combination of uppers and downers with enough liquor to lose depth perception. Thanks to the ecstasy in my system and the amphetamine-fueled sleep deprivation, it doesn't even register as awkward when she starts kissing me without saying anything. It is a little awkward, though, when her boyfriend walks in and she shoves away and wipes her mouth on her sleeve.

Syd says, "Hey, baby. This is my new friend."

He's higher than fuck himself, that or playing dumb. Either way, all he says is, "Hey, I'm Devon. I make moonshine." I expect him to pull a business card out, the way he says it. I kind of wish he would; that'd be pretty fucking surreal. He doesn't, though.

"Oh, that's dope," I say. "I ain't ever tried moonshine before."

"Man," he says, holding up an empty water bottle, "and I just killed the last of it. I'll bring you some next time."

I say, "Cool."

Syd and Devon leave together, arms around each other's waists. They close the door behind them. I tilt my head back and close my eyes for a minute. Seth's gurgled snores are muffled by the carpet against his face. The door flings open and smacks the wall and I jump halfway to the ceiling.

Jackie has one eye and a cocaine infatuation. The two are unrelated, I'm assuming (hoping)—just the first things I notice about her when she stumbles into the room, coughing violently and pounding her chest. She touches her temples. She says, "Hi, I'm Jackie." She reminds me of a pirate, but not because of the eye patch. She looks at my arms and neck and says, "You do those tatts yourself?"

I'm still standing on Earl's bed. I say, "Some. Mostly friends did them."

She says, "Same here," and extends her arms, decorated in stick figures and punk band logos and graffiti. She inhales sharply. Her one eye stays squinting and she sways on sea legs.

The last friendly name I learn tonight is Makayla, when she rushes in the room and ducks her shoulders under one of Jackie's arms and grabs her waist and tells her, "Let's go home, babe." To me, she says, "Sorry."

I shrug and hop off the bed. "Don't be," I say. "Everyone's getting gone tonight."

"Yeah," Makayla says as Jackie bites her ear, "some too far gone."

The party dies down a bit. Most of us chill on the back porch. Eric heats a gold plate of hash oil with a propane blowtorch. Sets the torch down next to the arm I'm leaning on, uncapping the Adderall to wake myself back up. This guy I don't know sits a little too close to me on the bench. I look up and he smiles—golden canines.

"You fiending, huh?" he says.

I look down at the backpack between his legs, say, "Why, what you got?"

"Shit, anything you need, man." He holds his hand out and says, "I'm Jermaine, I run all the dope within a dozen blocks of here."

I grip his hand to shake and he holds mine tight, leans in close enough so only I can hear him whisper, and I've just noticed looking over his shoulder the muscular friend he has with him.

"Here's what's going to happen," Jermaine says. "You're going to give me that bottle, you feel me? And I'll cut you in on a portion of the profits. You keep bringing me the pills and it's a win-win. Whatchu think, partner?"

I yank my hand away and say, "No, thanks, man."

Jermaine says, "Okay." Lifts his shirt to show the steel tucked in his jeans. "Then I'll just take it, huh?"

I tried being polite, but he pushed me, which took about as well as it ever does: not at all. He doesn't know me, though, so I can't say he should've seen it coming, but I also don't feel sorry when I tip Eric's blowtorch over and turn the nozzle, lighting the sleeve of Jermaine's hoodie on fire.

His friend carries him to the ground and falls on his arm,

rolling on it to put the flames out. Jermaine shouts, either about the fire or about his arm being crushed under his panic-stricken homeboy. I jump at the first opening I get and swipe the Glock from his waist.

Vyron, Trenton, Eric, Anthony, Rafael, Javi, and Ricardo all jump up and gather next to me. Vyron says, "The fuck happened?"

"Dumb bitch flashed a piece at me." My hands shake and my neck pulses. I can feel the adrenaline in my fingertips. I catch the fear in both their eyes down the sight of the heater. They stand frozen against the wall. I say, "This the reaction you were expecting from me?" I step close enough for Jermaine to feel the cold steel and my breath against the side of his face when I say, "This is what's going to happen: you don't fuck with me and I don't, well," I shrug, nod to the gun.

Jermaine's jaw tightens. He glares over the barrel. I can't help but smile.

"And I'm keeping your backpack. You feel me?"

His friend answers for him. "We'll leave y'all alone, a'ight?"

I step back so they can run away and jump the fence. Rafael has already dumped the bag out on the picnic table. Baggies full of you name it.

Vyron puts me in a headlock, kisses my head. "You're a muhfuckin' thug," he says.

"Just a little crazy," I say.

Rafael says, "What do we do with this shit?"

Vyron says, "That's up to baby boy."

"Fuck it," I say. "Take what you want. Anything left over, I'll sell."

We fill our pockets. I put what's left in the backpack and throw it onto the second-floor balcony next door. The guy who owns the house is locked up in prison on drug charges. I hide the heater in the bushes on his front porch. We go back to chilling like nothing happened.

HELENE

I have this dream where I'm floating in outer space, sniffing stardust off the rings of Saturn, and Helene—one of Saturn's sixty-something moons—hangs over my head, its surface cracking in a horizontal line and splitting open like a mouth with sharp rocks for teeth. The noise Helene makes when she inhales is the soundtrack of a head-on collision played backwards. She breathes me in and shuts her mouth. It's like a cave inside of her. I see everything in infrared night vision. I see myself sitting on a rock and when I notice me noticing myself, I look up from the rock with eyes that are all pupils and I speak in two voices at once: one voice dropped thirty octaves below normal, like chopped and screwed tone, the other a whispering echo. I tell myself, *the world as you know it is in your hands. The end of you is the end of it all.*

I watch myself vanish off the rock and I jerk awake with the feeling of falling.

NEW YEAR KISS

It's New Year's Eve and I have the kids, which means a weekend of regulating my speed consumption to just a few prescription Adderalls. It also means a queen size air mattress in my parents' living room and tiny feet in my ribcage all night. It also means a text from Vyron saying *we should throw a fucking rager tonight* and me texting back *can't, have the kids* and him texting back *damn, that sux* and me shutting my phone off.

Thanks to the burn ban, sparklers are the most we can get away with in the city limits. My dad lights the end of one and it sparks green and Deandre shouts "green means go!" and my dad hands him the sparkler and says "here, buddy, be careful" and Deandre chases Mitch and Brandon around the yard with it, tossing green sparks, shouting "green means go! Green means go!"

Destiny's pacifier bounces in her mouth. Serenity kneels down in front of her and lights a sparkler. Destiny's pacifier

21

drops to the ground. She flinches, taking the sparkler at arm's length and sword fighting the air with it. She makes a cute shriek/giggle noise and says "whoa, cool" in a baby lisp.

After we stomp out several colorful mini fires in the yard, my mom—being the only one able to do so—rocks Destiny to sleep, then Deandre clocks out after watching the same animated monster movie twice.

Anjelica doesn't sleep. She says her stomach hurts. I sit on the tub and rub her back while she sits doubled over on the toilet. Face between her knees, she says, "Grandma doesn't like my name." The kids call my mom Grams. Grandma would be Kim's mom. Anjelica says that Kim's mom, her grandma, thinks her name is ugly, that she said this to her. "That's why she calls me Annie," Anjelica says. "She thinks Annie is a pretty name for me."

A vein threatens to pop out my forehead and the heat rises under my skin. I swipe Anjelica's hair out of her face and crouch down so our eyes are level with each other and I hold my oldest baby's face in my hands and tell her she is a wonderful little girl and her name is beautiful, that everything about her is beautiful, and that her grandma is an ignorant, hateful cunt.

Anjelica squeezes my neck.

We spend the rest of the night on the couch with the back door open, watching the glow of fireworks going off outside the burn ban limits. Anjelica is lying on my chest. She looks up at me. Smiles. Kisses my cheek. Says, "You're the best daddy ever."

I hold her tight and hope she never stops believing that.

HEATHENISH

I'm lying sideways with my head in Vyron's lap, facing his stomach, and he's stretching the skin under my eye tight with his forefinger and thumb. His pupils are night owl big and the whites of his eyes are bloodshot. I know from catching a glimpse of myself in the mirror shard on the coffee table that mine look the same.

"You ready for this shit?" Vyron wields a pencil with an ink-dipped sewing needle wrapped around the eraser head.

Out of the twenty-something times I've offered my body as a graffiti canvas to friends, this will be my first stick-and-poke. "Do it, bitch."

"A'ight. You best stay awake and do mine, though. I'ma slap the fuck out of this fresh tattoo if you pass out."

Vyron pricks my face with the needle and draws into my skin with a sewing motion. My phone vibrates in my pocket and I pull it out and prop it against Vyron's stomach.

I read the blurry screen with one eye, the other clenched shut beneath the needle.

"Well," teeth gritted, hissed breathing, "I'm officially divorced."

Vyron pauses to slap me on the back and say, "Congratulations," then continues stabbing me in the face over and over with the tiny needle.

I feel light-headed. I say, "This is a fucking great night."

"We're making history on this couch, man," Vyron says.

"How's it looking?"

"It's looking dope. Be still."

I try to focus on breathing and imagine myself as stardust floating around in outer space until Vyron says "done" and drags what feels like a chunk of concrete but is really just a paper towel across my face, wiping up the blood and ink.

I roll off his lap and lean over the mirror shard and smile at the swollen inverted cross under my eye. "That's punk rock."

Vyron passes the needle. "Yeah, I fuck with it." He rolls up a pant leg. "Now tatt me up, you heathenish muhfucka."

There's a circle of us huddled under a tarp. Sideways rain mists our backs. Breath clouds circle our faces.

Vyron is balancing on one foot while holding up his freshly tatted ankle for everyone to see. He swings his fist through the air and stops before hitting the swollen, bleeding symbols that halo his white leather shoes, then he spreads his fingers and makes an explosive sound effect with his mouth. "That's my muhfuckin name in astrological symbols, muhfuckas."

Trenton takes a bud of dank from the plastic bag in Rafael's shaking hands and packs it in a cow bone engraved with hieroglyphics. He says, "Your name is Cocksucker?"

Vyron says, "As if your illiterate ass could read it if it did say that."

"I'm only dyslexic in English," Trenton says, holding the brass mouthpiece of the bone pipe to his lips and an eager bic flame above the bowl. "I'm fluent in astrological symbols, though. Your tattoo says 'Cocksucker.'"

"Pfft. You don't speak astrology, nigga."

The little hairs of the marijuana bud glow orange and spiral, burning. Trenton blows a dank fog and passes the bone to Rafael with both hands and they nod at each other as if *puff-puff-pass* is some sort of sacred ritual and in a way, I guess it is.

My phone vibrates. The name Sean—dollar sign for the *S*—lights up the screen. I hit the green button and put the phone against my ear in one quick motion and say, "How the fuck have you been?"

"Hey, little brother. It's been a minute. I's just calling to see what you up to. You still in Victoria?"

"Nah, I'm back in the 979. You still in Corpus Christi?"

"Man, I been in Wharton for a minute."

"Well, I haven't heard from you in forever. The fuck was I supposed to know?"

"Yeah, yeah, yeah," Sean says, "listen. I'ma be down— who's that talking? You with someone?"

"I'm with a few friends," I say. "There's several people talking."

"Pass the phone real quick."

"Huh?"

"Let me talk to your friend."

Vyron holds the bone pipe out in front of me and I trade him the phone for it. He asks me who it is as I inhale the dank and holding my breath, I say, "My brother."

Vyron puts the phone against his ear, says, "Um, hello?"

I open my mouth and let the smoke crawl out and pass the bone full circle to Trenton.

Vyron stutters some numbers to Sean with question marks in his voice and on his face. He says into the phone, "Uh, yeah, I couldn't tell you." Hands the phone to me, an eyebrow raised, says, "Your brother thinks I'm a drug dealer."

Sean says, "That nigga ain't a drug dealer."

I say, "I never said he was."

"My bad. Hey, listen, I've got some shit if you know of anyone interested down there. I can deliver, too—for a fee, of course."

"What kind of shit you got?"

"Shit." I can hear Sean smiling on the other end. "What

kind of shit you need? I got XOs, I got crystal, I got dro, I got powder. It's all high grade shit too. You know what I'm saying? Anything you need, I can get."

"Shit," I say, "I can sell just about anything down here." I wink at Vyron and say to Sean, "All my friends got vices."

Vyron nods, his ears exclusive to this side of the phone conversation.

Sean says, "You moving shit now?"

"You wanted to talk to a drug dealer," I say, "let's talk."

Sean says, "A'ight, look, I'ma be down next weekend and we can chill and I'll bring some shit if you got anyone interested."

"Cool."

"A'ight, love you."

"I love you, too."

Sean says, "Bet." Hangs up. I have no idea what that means, except for it's always how he's said goodbye.

Everyone hooks their chins up at the same time.

"You hoodrats want some shit?" I say.

Rafael says, "Kind of shit you got?"

I say, "What kind of shit you need?"

SON

Toys on the floor. Cartoons on the television. Kids taking turns dragging each other around in a box.

Serenity watches them play, her elbow on the arm of the couch, her chin in her hand, smile on her face. She says, "They look exactly like you."

I watch the animated ducks stow away on a rocket ship seconds from blastoff, reply to a text, write down a couple bars that just came to me. I say, "Huh?"

Serenity says, "The girls."

I say, "Oh, yeah. Lucky them, right?" I smile, then cringe. I touch my teeth and they all feel loose.

Serenity laughs at the kids laughing at each other and says, "They're like little girl clones of you."

It's true what she says. And it's true what she's not saying, about Deandre—how he more resembles Kim's brothers, and this guy I used to work with when I worked at the chemical plant.

28

Deandre decides it's his turn in the box, pushes it over. Anjelica tumbles out and face plants into the wall, begins sobbing.

I catch up to myself and realize I've gone too far after the handprint's started turning purple already.

I didn't mean to hit him that hard.

I swear I didn't.

At bedtime, Deandre wants to play a video game. I cave for once. I put in a violent one. I pick the sniper avatar. Deandre holds his controller upside down and his avatar runs in circles, aiming at the ground, dropping grenades that bounce wild. I pick a spot on a hill and blow his head off in my crosshairs. He respawns ten seconds later. I do it again. And again.

Deandre says, "I'm beating you, Daddy."

I turn the game off and clutch my stomach.

He says, "Why'd you turn it off?"

I say, "You win," and I roll over and lie down with my back to him.

I hear him drop to his pillow on his toddler bed. He whispers, "Goodnight, Daddy."

I bury my face in the sheets.

Deandre wakes up screaming in the middle of the night. He jumps in my bed, curls up against my ribcage like a chinchilla.

"Nightmare?" I say.

"Yes," he says, rubbing his eyes with little fists.

I rub his back in circles.

He says, "You're my boy, Daddy."

I say, "You're my boy. No matter what." I kiss his head and hold him close against my chest and whisper promises to him as he drifts to sleep.

SHADOWS EVERYWHERE

I eat a bunch of speed and decide to break into the neighbor's house. Along with the dirty penny taste of blood, a side effect of too much amphetamines seems to be these *fuck it* kind of impulses. I run my tongue over my teeth and cradle my jaw in my hand, swinging it left to right, making sure everything is still attached.

I jump the fence between Vyron's yard and the overgrown grass of the imprisoned drug dealer next door. Before he got raided and moved to a cell, he left the back door unlocked. The house reeks of mildew. There's asbestos in the walls and a jigsaw mess of broken glass on the carpet. I don't expect the police left any drugs or cash behind. I honestly can't say why I'm pulling all the drawers out, tossing all the mattresses over, other than a breaking-and-entering is something I've never done, so, fuck it.

Framed photos on the nightstand show the homeowner squeezing the jowls of a pit bull and puckering his lips in a kissing face at it/throwing the peace sign up with some friends gathered around a card table adorned with beers/ hugging an old lady with breathing tubes in her nostrils.

I feel like I know this stranger more than I should. I shouldn't be in his house.

There's a box of power tools that may go unused for several more years just sitting in his garage, though.

So, you know.

Fuck it.

I drag the box out the back door and lift/push it over the fence with a grunt. My head spins and I grip the metal fencepost for balance and notice the shadow creature with headlight eyes standing next to me. The shadow creature must have said something funny 'cause I catch myself laughing, but don't remember why. I blink several times and the shadow creature is gone and I think nothing else of it. I've been seeing shadows everywhere lately. When they start to fade is how I know it's time to dip into some more speed.

TODDLER DRUNK

Devon brings the moonshine he promised in a water bottle. It's bright red and smells like cinnamon and tastes like one of those fireball candies. It goes down smooth when I aim my chin at the stars and dome it, Vyron on one side of me shaking his head, saying, "No no no, you trying to kill yourself?" and Devon on the other side, slamming his fists on an invisible table and chanting *do it, do it, do it.*

The bottle crumples empty as I suck down the last of the shine. Devon cheers. Syd smiles and claps, then dips into a small baggy and sprinkles some powder over some reggie on a Zig Zag. Tonight, her mohawk is lime green.

The ground tilts forward and I throw my hands out, stumble side to side on sea legs.

Vyron says, "Let's get you inside, bro." He and Devon grab my arms and lead me inside. I break away from them when I see Seth and his girlfriend Holly on a couch in the living room, drinking and talking with a few hoodrats who showed up at a party here a couple days ago and never went home.

Holly smiles up at me, says, "Hey, it's been a while."

I lean over to give her a hug, end up falling on top of her. It's hard to speak when you can't feel your tongue, but I think I manage to ask how she's been.

She laughs, pats my back. "Has someone been drinking?"

Vyron says, "He's toddler drunk."

Devon says, "He domed a bottle of moonshine. First time he's ever tried it."

Seth shoves me off his girlfriend and I lie sideways next to them on the couch.

The rest of the night is pretty much me trying to get up and Seth shoving me back onto the couch. The time I do stand after slapping opposed hands away, I fall forward into Seth's mouth with my tongue. He tastes like cigarettes and brisket. I slide off his lap and he catches me less than an inch from face planting on the coffee table. Pulls me back onto the couch and says to stay laying down and I say, "Okay."

I check my phone. A text from a number I don't have saved says, *Hey, this is Kim's mom. I just wanted to say sorry for blaming you for everything. I see now you weren't the only one at fault.*

I put my phone in Seth's face and ask him what it says. He reads out loud what I thought I had read incorrectly.

I say, "Huh." I type a reply and ask Seth to read it before I hit send.

He laughs and says, "The only thing spelled correctly is 'cunt bitch.' Wait, no, you forgot the '*t*' in 'bitch.'"

I say, "Send it."

He says, "I'll save it to drafts and you can send it in the morning if you still want to." Seth tucks my phone in my pocket and covers me with a blanket. The room spins. My head rolls off the edge of the couch and Seth reaches over and pushes it back onto a pillow.

I smile at Holly, who's sitting on his lap now. I say, "It's so fucking good to see you. It's been so long."

She shakes her head, smiling. "Get some sleep."

I pass out and when I wake up the next morning, I'm the only one in the living room. I check my phone. I'm a couple hours late for work. I look at my texts on my way out the door and find the illegible saved draft and delete it.

I sit on the floor behind aisles of children's books and grab a toy from the plush tower and scan its bar code and drop it at my feet. Repeat the process until there's a shoulder-high plushy pile on either side of me.

A little girl opens a book at the kids' table in the corner. She smiles and waves at me. I wave back. Her mother power walks over and says, "Let's go, honey. You can read it in the car."

Vyron walks in and pulls up a child size chair and sits in it backwards. His tie is loose. I'm starting to think bloodshot is just part of his eye color. He says, "You look like death."

I say, "You look like you got fired."

"Nah." Vyron rowboats his shoulders, adjusting his jacket. He tightens his tie. "I always show up to work casually late."

I feel myself or the ground beneath me lean forward and my stomach swims laps around my other organs. I say, "I'm still a little drunk."

"You were toddler drunk last night, stumbling around like you forgot how to walk. You kept falling all over Holly, squeezing her tits. Lucky bastard."

"Is that why Seth kept shoving me?"

"He kept shoving you to keep you from cracking your damn skull open. Every time you stood up, you fell forward."

"I should call Holly. Apologize."

"She didn't think anything of it, man. She works at a fucking bar. She knows what drunk looks like."

"Still." I drop the scanner and put my head in my hands, try to massage the migraine out.

"How are you even functioning right now?"

"Speed," I say. "I think I'm addicted."

"Oh, I have no doubts you are, you fucking crank head." Vyron hooks his chin up, says, "What's that feel like—being high on that shit all the time?"

"You remember that feeling of jumping off a merry-go-'round when the kid spinning it seems like he's trying to either launch you into outer space or murder you?"

Vyron chuckles, eyes glistening as he stares off at nothing, montage of childhood playing in his head. He says, "Yeah."

I say, "I always have that feeling."

Vyron licks his lips and bites down on the bottom one. He looks over his shoulder. Rubs his chin. "You got any on you?"

I take the orange script bottle out of my pocket and shake it, toss it to him.

He smiles, says, "Baby boy," and pops the cap off. "How many can I take?"

I chunk deuces. He tilts the bottle, knocks two into his hand and puts them in his jacket pocket. Sets the bottle down in front of my legs crossed into lotus position. He slaps my shoulder and kisses my forehead, says, "Take it easy, brother," and he leaves to be thirteen minutes late for work.

I say, "You take it easy." Try offering a smile but it turns into a wince as phantom nails are driven through the front of my skull. I lay my head on a plush bearded dragon and rest my eyes until my name is called over the intercom.

TRY HARDER

Anjelica won't eat her dinner. She sits with her arms crossed, pouting at her plate.

I say, "You love chicken and rice. That's why Grams made it for you."

She shakes her head, pushes her plate across the table. I slide it back in front of her.

I say, "Eat."

She pushes herself up, gripping each of the wooden arm rests, so she's eye to eye with me when she screams in my face. My chair goes timber to the floor when I shove up from it to force Anjelica back into her booster seat. A door opens in the hallway and there's the sound of running water and Deandre playing in the tub and my mom asking what the hell is wrong with me as I'm shoving one fork-stabbed piece of chicken after another into Anjelica's mouth but instead of chewing or swallowing, she's crying with a mouthful of food until she chokes and coughs it up into her lap. She trembles and hyperventilates, stuttering out an apology. Over and over: "I'm sorry I'm sorry I'm sorry," still saying it when my mom pushes me aside and takes her up in her arms, carries her back to her bedroom and slams the door shut as the other bedroom doors open, heads poking out, question marks on all three of their faces.

Serenity crosses the hall and stands in the open doorway of the bathroom, says, "What are you doing?"

From inside the bathroom, a pacifier-muffled baby lisp: "Splashing Deandre."

Serenity shakes her head, smiling as she closes the door behind her to finish up Deandre's bath.

Dad and Brandon stand in the hall outside of Brandon's room, game controllers in their hands. Their eyes go from me to the coughed up chicken on the floor to the knocked over chair and back. I pick the chair up and my dad is standing next to me, asking what happened.

"I just want her to eat," I say. "I don't want her getting sick. It's never been a struggle with her before."

"Things aren't like before," Dad says. "I understand the frustration, but we have to be patient with each other. It's an adjustment for all of us, the kids too, and you've got to remember Anjelica is only three. She's been through a lot in the small amount of time she's been here—been alive, I mean. She's very smart, but she's not grown up. She's just a baby."

I nod my head, *yeah, I know,* trying not to choke on the lump in my throat.

She is just a baby still, and knowing her—what we've been through together in her three years—tomorrow, I'll sit her in my lap and drive around the backyard and she'll be wearing my sunglasses upside down on her face and she'll cradle my chin in a hand too small to grip the steering wheel and say I'm the best daddy in the whole wide world.

Tonight, though, I'm the worst.

I hear sobs from the hall as I make my way to turning the door knob slow and inching inside, head hung low seeing my baby soaked in tears I've precipitated.

My mom glares. Anjelica looks up from her lap with wet, kicked puppy eyes. Between each panic breath she sucks in, Anjelica gets a word out. She fumbles out an "I... love... you" with a sob sucked in between each word. I sit on the edge of the bed and hold my hands out and she jumps from my mom's arms to mine. She buries her face in my chest and swings little right hooks into my ribcage.

I stroke her hair and say I'm sorry—so, so sorry—and I hope the fact that I'll be saying it until the world ends doesn't dilute the sincerity in this moment. I draw finger circles on her back and say, "I'm trying to do things right. I'm trying to be the best dad in the world for you."

Anjelica stops punching me in the ribs and wipes her tears and snot on my shirt. She looks up at me, says, "Try harder." Then she closes her eyes against me, and I channel all the thoughts I can't articulate into my chest, hoping the rhythm of my heartbeat speaks to her somehow, says the right words that I could never say.

BLACK TAR

I've tried to kill myself something like six times before but the one time I succeed is a total accident.

It's the first time I try heroin.

It's the last time I try heroin.

The old man sitting shotgun points at a house with tinfoil in the windows. Says, "This is it."

I whip the Jeep with dealership tags too hard to the right and hop the curb.

The hunchback says, "Wait here." He slides off the seat and drops to the driveway with a grunt. Straightens his tie.

A woman at least half his age cradles an infant in a rocking chair on the porch. The old man kisses them both before disappearing inside.

The woman is barefoot. Nails painted all different neon colors. Cut-off jeans and a tank top suggest she has no skin to spare for more ink.

The baby grabbing at her bleached dreadlocks is naked. The baby has no tattoos.

The woman smiles gap-toothed at her baby and makes motorboat sounds while tickling her tummy. Moves her motor lips closer and closer to her face. Touches her motor lips to her skin. The baby giggles and does street fighter moves in her mother's lap.

The old hunchback comes back out the house and kisses them again and uses the oh shit handle to pull himself into the Jeep.

He drops a balloon and a small plastic coffin in the cup holder. Says, "150."

I stretch the balloon open under my nose and make a face that makes the old man chuckle.

"Smells like vinegar."

"It's good shit."

"How much for the syringe?"

The old man shakes his head and backhands the air. "I've got access to a fuck-load of needles," he says. "My son's a diabetic."

My heart trades places with my throat trades places with my stomach and I turn my head so the old man doesn't see my disgust at the revelation he's a parasitic deadbeat, or the deeper disgust in myself for being no different.

I want to tell his wife and children they deserve better.

I want to be the better that someone else deserves, that my own kids deserve.

I want to stop feeling like a piece of shit.

I want some fucking smack to make this feeling go away.

I set the money on the console and the old man's leather face cracks a smile and I drive the Jeep back to the dealership and the old man shakes my hand and says it's a pleasure and asks what I think of the Jeep and I pocket the skag balloon and needle coffin and tell him it handles horribly and it's too fucking big. He says he'll see me again soon, then he joins the other car salesmen smoking on the patio.

Vyron is with them and looks at me like he's just seen a stranger who reminded him of a long-lost loved one. His face in my rearview is as if he's watching a close friend being lowered into a grave. I decide to shoot up in Vyron's bathroom so in case I fuck it up, he'll be home in a few hours to take care of me because he's the best friend I have in this world.

I stretch the lip of the balloon and shake the black tar out onto the sink. Cut a chunk off with a quarter. Run a thin stream from the faucet. Drop the chunk of smack in a rusty spoon. Hold the spoon under the faucet for a split second. Tear a small cloud off a cotton ball and drop it in the brown spoon water. Set the spoon down gently on the back of the toilet. Take the lace from my left shoe, tie it above my elbow. Open the plastic coffin and sit on the toilet, syringe in one shaking hand, spoonful of heroin in the other. Stab the puffed up cotton with the needle and suck the shit into the chamber.

The ritual of shooting up for the first time feels like joining a religion.

I fuck up on the first try. Before even slamming the shit in, I stab the crook of my elbow too hard and blow the vein out. I drag the needle back out and search the bluish green branches on my arm for another promising one. I find it in my wrist. This time I don't fuck it up and an orgasmic rush explodes from the core of my body and rattles my spine and my arms and legs grow heavy.

It's like starting to sink with no fear of drowning to death.

It's like being a rocket as it blasts off into space and then just floats before the fall back to earth.

It's the closest I've ever felt to god.

And now the world is dark. I am alone and empty and detached from my body. I'm okay with death at first. I embrace it like a soft blanket. After a while though, it feels a lot like suffocating, like my chest is caving in and my lungs are about to blow.

I'm pulled from the abyss back into my shell slumped on the floor against the toilet.

I hear a hard smack and feel a sting on the side of my face that will linger forever. Sweat splatters the flowers on the wallpaper. Vyron is crouched over my legs, gripping my shirt, slapping my face side to side, screaming at me: *wake the fuck up motherfucker you can't be dead fuck you fucking breathe quit being a bitch and breathe!*

I look up to the ceiling and feel his mouth around mine, him breathing into me.

He punches me in the chest and I cough in his face and he kisses my head and squeezes my neck.

I say, "I'm going to puke."

Vyron backs off and sits in the corner and I turn my head and vomit what looks like blood and coffee grounds on top of the toilet seat. I still can't move my arms.

Vyron sits in the corner, eyes wide/lips quivering. He wipes sweat from his forehead and loosens his tie. Says, "You were fucking dead."

My face spasms as I try to smile and wink. My breath rattles. I say, "I'm invincible, baby. Ha."

Vyron doesn't laugh. Even when I vomit again on his shoes, he just sits in the corner, reiterating that I was dead—that I was fucking *dead*, man—shaking his head in his hands, not thinking any of this is funny.

WAR TOWN

Sean pulls up in a box frame Cadillac and has his girlfriend pop the trunk for me to throw my backpack in, then he tells her to hop in the back with the kids so I can ride shotgun. I say, "You don't have to," but she says, "No, it's fine," and tells the little girl to scoot.

Sean's girl and her two kids—a son and a daughter, eleven and seven—I'll never forget their names, no matter what happens to them, 'cause before we ride out to Wharton, we make a stop at Sean's friend Dwayne's house, where—lying on a fold-out massage bed in the dining room—Sean gets their names etched in his skin. Lexi, Cameron, Meghan. It's Dwayne's idea for them to sign their own names on the stencil paper. He wields the razor and the Speed Stick, bites a corner of his lip, searches for unstained flesh on Sean's torso.

"Damn, bro," Dwayne says, "you get all this ink when you was locked up?"

Sean says, "Yeah. Wasn't nothing better to do." He explains how they made ink out of cigarette ash and charcoal and shampoo, shook it together in prescription bottles for hours until it was blended well enough, and how they stole telephone wire and stripped outlet boxes from the ceiling to make the guns and the needles. "Each one took months," he says, holding out arms covered in distorted, withering faces—their mouths agape, their eyes either hollow or bulging. "I told the dude that did it that I just wanted some evil shit and let him do his thing."

"Looks evil," Dwayne says. "So where should I put the kids' names?"

Sean finds enough empty space under his right arm for Meghan and in the crook of his left elbow for Cameron and that's where they'll be forever. For Lexi, he looks at me and says, "Well, since this punk had to go and get his fucking neck all tatted up, and I don't even have a neck tattoo, I guess that's where it's going."

He lies on his back on the massage bed. His foot twitches when Dwayne gets to the *x* over his carotid artery. He groans, bites down on his shirt. He says, "I fucking hate you right now."

I say, "I didn't tell you to do it."

"You didn't say it'd hurt like this either."

"It's a tattoo, you dumb shit. Since you're copying everything I do, I'ma get dollar signs next." I close my eyes and touch two fingers to my eyelids. "Right here."

Sean says, "Fuck you."

Dwayne snickers, wipes bloody ink off Sean's neck. The gun buzzes.

Lexi checks her phone. She says, "I'm going to visit a friend while you finish here."

"The fuck?" Sean says. "Who?"

Dwayne says, "Shit, man, don't move."

Lexi says, "I'll be right down the road. I'm taking the car. Text me when you're done." She leaves without the kids.

I say, "I didn't get a bitch's name on my neck either."

When Lexi brings the car back, her pupils are dilated. She leaves the engine running and hops in the back. Wipes her nose on her wrist.

Sean swings her door open, almost off its hinges, and slams a fist on top of the car. He smiles and puts his neck so close to her face she has to slide away from him to focus. He says, "See that?" His teeth stay clenched in a grin when he says, "You gotta love me forever now."

Lexi says, "I didn't tell you to get my name tatted on your neck."

Meghan hums, Cameron snores, and their mother sniffs and exhales, but other than that, the backseat is quiet all the way to Wharton.

Sean tells more stories of prison. "It was pretty dope sometimes," he says. "I just got bored as fuck."

48

* * *

Sean pulls into a gravel driveway, parks the Cadillac behind his truck. He says, "Home sweet home," and everyone shuffles up the steps to the trailer. One bedroom, one bathroom. I get the grand tour from the front porch.

Sean tucks the kids in on their cots. They call him dad. They say, "Goodnight, dad," and, "I love you, dad," and he says, "Goodnight, my angels," and kisses their foreheads. Then he slaps Lexi's ass and says, "Night, babe," and she mumbles something with her face wrapped up in the sheets.

Sean tosses me an extra hoodie from the closet that touches my knees and hangs loose on my frame. We sit in his truck with the engine off and the windows up, freezing. He reaches in the glove box and pulls out a gram of dro. We sit and smoke it out of a red white and blue pipe. I spark the grass every time I breathe in. Sean drums two fingers over the bowl to keep it burning. He says, "I never thought I'd be smoking weed with you one day. You were a squeaky clean church kid. What happened?"

I almost blow a smoke ring. "I got older," I say.

Sean sighs. He looks through the frost on the window at the trailer. He says, "I don't want to go in." The letters of the fresh tattoo are raised on his neck, already scabbing.

I say, "Why are you with her?"

"I don't know. I like the crazy bitches."

"You're alone on that."

"Lexi's okay. I mean, I love her, you know."

"Whatever makes you happy."

Sean coughs. Raises the pipe. "This," he says. "This makes me happy. And XOs, and crystal, and lean, and money and guns and fast cars. And fucking crazy bitches." He laughs and has another coughing spell. Pounds his fist against his chest. "That's what makes me happy."

In the morning, I wake to the smell of bacon and eggs, and to Sean marching out the door—cigarette between his teeth, phone against his ear. I eat breakfast with Lexi and the kids and help with the dishes. Sean comes back in and eats out of the skillet and grabs a beer from the fridge. He kisses Lexi's cheek and tells her we'll be back whenever and taps me on the shoulder and says, "Let's go."

On our way down the steps, I ask where we're going.

Sean says, "We smoked the last of the dro last night. We're going to get some more."

We stop at Jack in the Box and Sean sends a text. A few minutes later, a Coupe de Ville creeps through the parking lot twice around before hitting the drive-thru and parking next to us. Sean gets out and talks to the driver. A guy from the backseat of the de Ville hops out and taps on my window. I roll it down. He asks for a cigarette, eyes darting all over the cab. I say I don't have one, and he says, "Open the door and show me."

When I open the door, he jumps back a bit, hands

crossed in front of him, ready to draw heat. I hold my hands out, palms up. Motion around the inside of the truck.

"See," I say. "Nada."

The gang banger is satisfied. He returns to the de Ville.

Sean returns to the truck with a to-go bag. He hands the bag to me. It's full of dro.

Sean says, "Now, we can't smoke all that, even though I'd love to. I need to make at least three hundred off of it. We can smoke a good little bit, though."

Sean smiles. He waves at the gang bangers pulling out. One waves back.

We drive around the city. Sunlight fractures through the twisted limbs of dead trees. Rows of headstones stretch to the horizon. You can almost hear the foundation crack beneath dilapidated homes and businesses. Sean parks out front of a closed body shop at a fork in the road. We sit and listen to music and don't speak for a long time. I watch a spider crawl across the dashboard. Sean turns the music down and the truck stops vibrating. He says, "Sometimes, I drive around all day, just to get away from everything. I don't smoke or answer my phone—nothing. I shut myself off from the world until I'm ready to go back to it."

Cars go by.

A dog with mud caked to its paws walks up and pisses on the front passenger side tire, then runs across the road and disappears in a wheat field.

Sean says, "You want to see the house we're working on?"

I say, "Sure."

The house we pull up to is lit up by flashing reds and blues. The neighbor across the street is tackled in the yard by a couple of cops. They kick him in the head before shoving him in the back of one of their squad cars—bloody, barefoot, and in his boxers.

I follow Sean around to the back door. He says, "Ain't nothing but fiends and thugs all up and down this street. It's never boring." He unlocks the door and goes through the house, flipping lights on. There's two bedrooms and two bathrooms and a washer and dryer hooked up and a fridge and a range oven and a couch and a television.

I say, "So, why the fuck are y'all living in a trailer?"

Sean points to a stack of wood floor tiles. "Lexi wants the floor finished first. I do a little bit at a time so I can come here and have a place to chill out when we fight."

We sit on the couch and Sean turns on the television and packs a bowl.

I say, "Are you fighting right now?"

He shrugs.

We smoke the pot and watch cartoons.

I notice Sean's asleep when he stops chuckling.

I cash the bowl.

Sean's phone buzzes on the cushion between us, the screen covered in unread texts and missed calls from Lexi.

I go to take a piss and the toilet doesn't flush and at first I think, *the fuck?*, but then I get excited and hopeful when lifting the lid on the tank, and sure enough, there's a big bag of crystal. I eat a knuckle-sized rock and my eyes loosen in my skull and I can feel my hair growing.

Sean is on the back porch, shouting on the phone when I come out of the bathroom. I don't know what to do, so I do some push-ups, then I lay half the floor in the kitchen and then stand in the middle of the living room, staring at the television—zoomed in on the lights behind the screen.

Sean slams the door behind him when he comes storming through the house, flipping all the lights off. He says, "Let's go."

In the truck, he says, "You've always had it made."

I say, "The fuck are you talking about?"

"You ain't got the shit to worry about like I do."

I say, "One time, I held a gun to my head. It was the most relaxed I've ever been in my life. In that moment, the world was in my hands; I was in control. I was so relaxed, all the knots around my spine loosened up and my legs went numb and I fell asleep. When I woke up, I didn't feel like ending it anymore, at least for the rest of the day. I got by for a little while longer. Some shit you bring upon yourself and sometimes the world just takes a huge shit on you but for the most part, problems are a part of your DNA. I was born a little fucked up in the head. I'm addicted to addictions. I'm like my own fucking parasite. Don't tell me I don't have worries, or I don't understand. I understand a lot."

"We're pretty fucked up, huh?" Sean says. "I think we have a sickness."

"We are a sickness."

When we get back to the trailer, it's screaming and cussing and slamming doors and then it's cots being moved into the living room and the creaking of bedsprings through thin walls.

Meghan and Cameron max the volume on the television in an attempt to drown out their mother's *fuck me* chants, but it doesn't work, and what's worse than hearing your brother's sex moans or the obnoxious laughter of an animated sponge is being caught between both at the same time.

Sean flicks my ear to wake me up at three in the morning so I can get home, shower, and drive myself to work. He grabs a couple beers for the road. Both are his. A couple miles down a farm road, he pulls over and packs a bowl and we smoke it 'til it's cashed. He scratches at the name in blistered ink on his neck.

He says, "I hate that bitch."

I say, "So leave. You deserve better than that."

"I love her, too, though. And the kids."

"You're not their dad."

"I'm the closest they've ever had. It ain't about blood, you know."

"Yeah. I know."

"I'll leave sooner or later, probably. Maybe we'll be

together forever, but probably not. I don't know. It always takes longer than it should to walk away. You get comfortable, you know."

"Or complacent."

"It's like what you said last night—about being addicted and shit. I got lots of addictions that are bad for my health, and that bitch is one of them."

Sean turns his hazards off and gets back on the road. We roll the windows down to let the smoke blow out.

DRIFTING

"Soon as I get in the backseat of that taxi," Javi says, "it's fucking *on*. There's going to be lots of this," Javi makes his hands into claws and holds them at his chest, "a fuckload of this," he wraps his arms around an invisible woman, closes his eyes, wiggles his tongue around, "and maybe even some of this," he sticks his tongue between two fingers spread to make a *V*, "before we even get home. Every time I've jacked off since I've been gone, I've put a dollar in a jar, saving up for that poor cab driver's tip."

Vyron says, "How long's it been now?"

Javi says, "Two years."

Ricardo shakes his head, says, "That cabbie will be able to retire off of your tip."

"Hold up," Vyron says. "You been away for two years, working and sending paper home to your girl in Mexico, and Handy Manny's the only action you've had?"

"Correct, sir," Javi says, toking a blunt.

"We might generally be pieces of shit," Ricardo says, tuning his guitar, "but my brother and I were raised to be loyal people."

Vyron says, "Couldn't do it." Shakes his head slow. Puts a double cup of lean to his lips and upon noticing it empty, takes a sip from mine.

My head swims.

Makayla says, "I respect that a lot, actually." She holds her Strawberita out over the picnic table and Javi touches it with the rim of his 40, says, "Gracias, señorita."

The back door swings open, the knob punching a hole in the drywall, and Jackie sways over to where Makayla sits with her legs against her chest. She grabs Makayla's face with both hands and kisses her deep. Makayla's heels dig into the bench and her face turns red. Jackie peels her face away, licking her lips as she does, and clouds dance around Makayla's face as she sucks in oxygen.

Jackie staggers off the porch and stands over the cardboard-burning fire barrel in the yard.

I put a hand on Makayla's shin and she kicks my arm away. "Sorry," she says. "Reflex."

I shake my head and make a face in a *don't sweat it* type of way and ask if she's alright.

It's quiet enough at the table to hear the sticks popping in Javi's trash weed as he takes a long drag on the Swisher.

"She's better—" Makayla says about Jackie, who's grinding her ass down the fire barrel, knees gripped, "she's better when she's not coked out."

Jackie shrugs her leather jacket off her shoulders and lets it slide off onto the frost-tipped grass blades.

"When she's sober," Makayla says, "she's very sweet."

Jackie exposes her back to the fire—arms crossed, pulling her Bettie Page t-shirt off over her head. The flames reflected in her sweat look like shooting stars sliding down her skin. She wraps her shirt around a stick and dips it in the fire. Runs around the yard pumping the t-shirt torch and howling at the moon.

Vyron gets up from the bench with a sigh and steps in front of Jackie, hooking an arm around her waist and yanking the torch from her grip. He throws the torch on the porch and stomps it out. Jackie falls face first into his chest, hands clapped on his shoulders. Her spine jumps up and down with her cries.

She says, "That was my favorite shirt."

Vyron gets the arms, I get the legs. We carry passed-out Jackie to the couch and cover her with her leather jacket.

Makayla asks Javi and Ricardo to drop her off at a friend's house before they head home and the three of them say goodnight and we all wish Javi good luck in Mexico.

Vyron says, "I'ma clock out." He points at Jackie with his head. "Wake me up if she's too much for you to handle tonight."

I say, "I'm sure she'll be fine," even though I'm not so sure.

* * *

Jackie snores. I pick at someone's acoustic guitar on the love seat.

When it's dark dark outside, Jackie springs to her combat boots and sways with her head in her hands. She motions with her head for me to scoot over so when she takes the cushion next to me, I'm on her blind side. I set the guitar in her lap and she says "thank you" and plays old country and grunge songs.

I can't see her eye, but it's in the way her cheekbone juts out, in the paper thin tightness in her neck.

"Makayla loves you," I say, "she just wants you to get better."

Jackie whispers, "I know," and I drift off to her playing and singing a Leadbelly song the way Kurt Cobain would.

Jackie's gone when I open my eyes. Only the guitar sits on the cushion next to me. Syd lays her head sideways on her arms crossed over the back of the couch. Today, her mohawk is the color of a crow.

She says, "You're cute when you're fucked up."

I say, "You're just fucked up."

She bites her lip in a smirk and shrugs.

PUNK ROCK FREDDIE'S BIRTHDAY

It's Punk Rock Freddie's birthday and there's a party being thrown for him at the Sixth Ave house. Punk band t-shirts and ripped jeans with suspenders and plaid skirts with fish-netted legs and combat boots everywhere, like a circus freak militia has invaded the place.

This is Earl's crowd. I can fuck with it.

A woman draws an icing pentagram on a Boston cream pie. Her t-shirt is scissored in half. Tattoo of Baphomet on her stomach.

I ask her where the birthday boy is.

She says, "Back porch. You know my brother?"

"We used to go to the same concerts," I say. "Jammed together a few times."

"Oh, cool. I'm Haley."

I tell her my name and we shake hands and the piercings in her cheeks double her dimples when she smiles.

On my way to the back door, Vyron stumbles in front of me, a girl under each arm barely holding him up—one wearing his blazer, the other his tie. Vyron is slicked with sweat, has Clint Eastwood eyes. He says, "You want to tag team?"

I say, "No, thanks."

He says, "Hey, give me some speed."

I dig my prescription bottle out of my pocket and tilt a tablet out into my hand. Drop it in the breast pocket of his blazer. The girl wearing it, her eyes are closed and a smile is spread across her face, like she's asleep and having the best dream ever.

Vyron licks his teeth and grits them, says, "Yuh, nigga."

The threesome disappears down the hall, rocking this way and that, somehow holding each other up.

The back porch punks toast their beers to the moon; dance and sing along to Misfits' *Static Age* blaring distorted from the stereo perched on the window sill. Punk Rock Freddie is leaning against the broken hot tub, nodding his head to the music and smiling at everyone enjoying themselves. I walk up to him and before I can get the "irth" in "happy birthday" out, he bear hugs me and says, "It's been forever, man. Thanks for coming to my party." We lean back against the hot tub, the brown leaves on the cover crunching under our elbows.

He pendulum swings a long, yellow fingernail across his throat and says, "I like the ink."

"Thanks," I say. "My little sister did all the work on my neck."

"That's cool. I like the phonograph."

"I'll let her know. You've got some wicked job killers."

"Which ones?"

I follow the trail of ink from the triple six above his right eyebrow to the red-eyed wolf over his carotid artery to the sleeves of double-headed dogs and pitchforked devils and jack-o' lanterns to the goat head on one hand and pentagram on the other and I tell Freddie, "All of them."

He chuckles. Says, "So how old are you now?"

"Twenty," I say. "You?"

"Thirty-eight today, my friend. And only getting younger. It's like, life is just recently getting started for me, you know. I've got the partying shit out of my system, no more probation shit to deal with, an okay gig riding a garbage truck. You know, picking up trash and chunking it in the compressor." His lips purse and move to the left side of his mouth and he shrugs. "It's whatever. When I'm not working, I just hang out. I like to be surrounded by people I care about. Trying to put a band together. You still play?"

"I still play guitar sometimes. I mostly rap as of late, though."

"Hey, man, music is music. We should get together and jam sometime."

"Fuck yeah," I say.

Makayla stands on top of the picnic table, holds her

phone over her head, shouts over the music. "Freddie! It's Jackie!"

Freddie points from Earl to the stereo, says, "Kill that for a second."

Earl runs over and mutes the music and everyone gathers in front of Makayla, who says "okay, ready" into her phone and extends her arm above the crowd of colorful spiked hair. On speaker, Jackie recites a poem for Punk Rock Freddie. Haley brings the cake out, Disney princess candles lit above the 666 and pentagram drawn in icing. Jackie finishes her poem with a happy birthday wish and Freddie blows out the candles.

Jackie says, "I wish I was there. I'll be out of rehab in six weeks."

Freddie says, "Get better, sweetheart. I'm so proud of you."

Makayla says, "We all are. I love you, babe."

"Love you, too."

Punk Rock Freddie dries his eyes with his knuckles and grins, says, "I love all of you, from the bottom of my heart." He spins a circle, says, "I sincerely love you all."

Jackie says, "Someone raise a tall boy for me. To you, Punk Rock Freddie."

The punks raise their drinks in a Lady Liberty fashion and parrot, "To Punk Rock Freddie!"

WILL

Vyron calls me at work, says to meet him at the dealership when I get off. His voice is hoarse. I say, "Okay."

When my shift is over, I drive next door and find Vyron's office and pull a chair out from his desk. Vyron stands as I sit. He shakes his head and says, "Let's go outside."

Behind the building, he smacks a pack of American Spirits in his palm and breaks the seal. He pulls one out with his teeth and holds the pack out for me to take one and sets it down on the hood of a random Mustang. His hands shake. I light both our cigarettes.

I ask what's wrong.

Vyron looks at the ground, shuffles his feet. He sucks his cig to the filter without a word. Puts another between his teeth for me to light. Says, "What are you up to today?"

I say, "Kim texted me, said she invited Seth over to hang out while her parents are out of town looking for a place to move, and she said she got blackout drunk and woke up in bed wearing different clothes and the house was all a mess, like, shit was broken on the floor from being knocked off the walls or pushed off end tables, and she found Seth's underwear on top of hers in the shower and the curtain rod on the floor. So I texted Seth, told him what I'd heard, asked if it was true—you know how Kim likes to start shit for attention—and now I'm waiting on his reply to determine what I'ma do next: if I just ignore it—'cause why the fuck should I care?—or if I break his legs."

Vyron turns his head to blow smoke, then says, "The fuck you care either way for? She's a hoe, and Seth is scummy." He shrugs. "So what?"

"She had the kids, for one," I say. "This all went down when they were sleeping, sure, but." I take a long drag and blow the smoke out my nose. "That just doesn't sit right with me. Kinda makes me sick, actually. Plus, I think Holly should know if her man is out getting drunk with single moms and fucking them while their kids are home. She's too good a person to put up with that shit."

Vyron nods. Stares up at the clouds. Blows smoke.

I break the silence. "So what, man, you just wanted to see my pretty face on your long-ass smoke break?"

Vyron's smile fades as soon as it shows up. He says, "You know Will? Always hanging out on the patio where you work, wears a leather jacket even when it's mid summer?"

I say, "Yeah, I know Will. Everybody knows Will. Why, what's up?"

It takes another cigarette for Vyron to get the words out. I can't believe what I hear.

Will's the kind of guy who reads Physics textbooks for fun, but has never been to college except to hang out on campus. If a friend asked him for a dollar to get a drink or a snack, he'd insist on giving everything in his wallet and explain how he never wants to see someone he cares about go hungry. He only ever raises his voice at his older brother. He holds doors open for fat chicks. He's never thrown a fist, but he'd kill for his family. His weathered face and thick beard make him look fifty, but he's barely three years older than me. And now, he has cancer.

"In his blood," Vyron says.

"Fuck, man."

Vyron shakes his head. His shoulders slump under the weight of the world that's been dropped upon them. He says, "Bruh, it's bad. Like, he's fucked. The hospital let him go home so he can die in his own bed. I'ma go say what's up to him this evening, if you want to come with."

"Yeah," I say. "Just let me know."

We drop the last of the Spirit sticks to the ground and stomp out the embers. We exhale in harmony, leaning back against the wall and staring at the clouds, which have all turned grey.

Will is a bedridden paper mâché skeleton who doesn't so much breathe as he gasps for air. His skin is stretched communion wafer thin, so whether he's smiling or cringing in pain, his face doesn't change. He doesn't talk a lot, but every time Vyron is quiet for longer than a few seconds, Will extends a boney finger and pokes his cheek, prodding him to keep talking. Lightened up versions of the hoodrat shit we've been up to seem to be Will's only source of entertainment.

I only know all this because Vyron says as much, pacing around the back porch and trying to swallow the knots in his throat. Instead of taking the last chance I'd ever get to kick it with Will, I spent the afternoon with Seth, killing a bottle of Sailor Jerry and playing *Grand Theft Auto V* after getting the shit with Kim straightened out. When I brought it up to him at his front door, Seth said, "Does that sound like me?" and I shrugged, shook my head no, and that was the end of it as far as we were concerned.

A trip to the corner store for some Colt 45s and a freestyle session to a DJ Screw CD later, we're on Vyron's back porch getting the low down on just how fucked Will is.

I take a pull from a 40. I ask Vyron when he's going to see him again. "I'll go with you," I say.

He says, "Don't worry 'bout it. His family ain't taking no more visitors. His moms told me they didn't mind me going 'cause Will saw us as brothers. I didn't know that shit. I mean, we hung out sometimes, yeah. We'd play shooter games online and cuss out little bitch-ass kids over the headsets, or I'd set up my laptop and drum machine and Will would try to put together some beats, even though his honky ass had the rhythm of a braindead gorilla. He'd get lucky with it sometimes, though. Some of his shit sounded pretty dope. Weird as fuck, like Clams Casino on acid, but dope. I'm glad I kept all of it now, even the whack shit." Vyron snatches the 40 from my hands and when he hands it back, it's nothing but witch piss. He wipes the foam off his lip and says, "I never knew he thought we was brothers, though. Guess you never know the impact you leave on someone 'til it don't make a fucking difference anymore."

Later on in the night, I make an impact on the ground with my face. My cheek goes from ice cold to blood warm.

Makayla says, "Shit. Are you okay?"

Seth answers for me. "He goes hard like that all the time. See, his eyes ain't rolled back in his head or nothing. He's good. Fucked up as he is, he probably didn't feel shit."

I want to tell Seth how wrong he is, but my tongue is numb. That, or I bit it off when my chin hit the concrete. Hours later, when everyone else goes home, it's the first thing I check. Before pushing myself up and peeling the raw meat side of my face off the sticky blood spatter, I put my fingers in my mouth and breathe a sigh of relief.

Vyron comes out with a cigarette in his mouth and catches me climbing into the drained hot tub, pauses with his hand cupped around the lighter at his face. "Mind if I join you?" he says.

I slap the space next to me on the bench seat and Vyron climbs in and hands me a cigarette. Once again, I'm lighting up for both of us 'cause of how bad his hands are shaking.

He takes a long drag and says, "Will is dead."

I don't know what to say to that, so we sit and smoke in the dry hot tub without saying another word. The only sounds are the locusts and the two of us trying not to cry out loud.

The day before Will's funeral, I get a text from Vyron saying he got his commission check off this expensive car that he sold and that he's treating us out some place nice tonight. So when he pulls in to the drive thru at McDonald's, I'm all like, "what the fuck?" and he looks at me with this innocent face like, "what? The fuck you want, nigga?" and I decide to drop it and tell him I'll have a spicy chicken sandwich, plain and dry.

He says, "That's gross," and to the monotone intercom that asks for our order, he says, "Yeah, give me a spicy chicken sandwich, but don't put any shit on it, and give me four double cheeseburgers with everything."

The chick at the window rolls her eyes at us, or maybe the bass bumping from the car, or yeah, maybe just us—red-ringed irises and sweat dotted foreheads.

Vyron says, "What, bitch? You work at McDonald's." He burns out of the exit and whips the Altima onto the highway. Scarfs down his fourth double before I even take a bite of the cardboard bread and spongey chicken. Mouthful of dollar menu burgers, he says, "Devon told me you been hanging out with Syd."

I shrug. "I mean, I smoked some crystal with her."

"Yeah?" Vyron smiles the way I imagine the devil will when he greets me at the gate. He says, "Baby boy smoking meth and getting that pussy?"

"God, no. She just always has hard drugs laying around."

"Good. That hoe is a fucking sociopath. She'd probably force you to come inside her so you knock her up and then she'd get an abortion."

"The fuck?"

"I'm only telling you shit that's happened before."

"Nah," I say. "I do have a shred of self-respect. I never touched her."

"That's good," Vyron says. "Don't."

We stop at a liquor store. I wait out in the car since I'm underage. I watch Vyron through the barred glass door vomit all over the linoleum and I laugh until I can't breathe. When he's thrown a mop and a yellow bucket, I slam my fist on the dash and feel the tears roll down my face.

Vyron cleans up his sick and browses the aisles like nothing happened, looking only at the top shelves. He returns to the car with two brown bags under his arms and we head back to the house and empty six bottles of different flavored Ciroc in a large pot. We fill a 16 oz cup and pour it out in the yard for Will and drink three liters between the two of us before we pass out. In the morning, we crush some speed with an empty bottle and I cut four lines on the coffee table mirror. Vyron says he's good after one bump, so I touch noses with my reflection a third time. I tilt my head back and count the seconds between each pulse in the ceiling.

While Vyron changes into his pallbearer suit, I juggle the six empty bottles on the back porch. Then I sweep up the broken glass. Then I take the bottom E string out of one of Earl's guitars hanging on a wall in the sun room and I bend the string around my neck and pull each end in opposite directions and just when I start to feel light headed, Vyron slaps my wrist and says, "Don't make today be about two dead homies."

In the parking lot of the Catholic church, we check ourselves in the sun visors. Wipe the blue residue off our noses with our wrists.

Vyron takes a deep breath. He says, "You ready?"

I say, "Are you?"

He shakes his head.

A few seconds later, we go inside. Vyron walks to the open casket and puts his hands on the edge and leans in. He walks back drying his eyes on his sleeve. Says, "He looks good. He's wearing his leather jacket."

My throat in a knot, I say, "That's good. I don't want to see."

Vyron nods like he understands and he stares up at the stained glass windows and sucks his bottom lip in. His eyes glisten. I throw my arms around him and there in the middle of the aisle, we hold each other and try not to lose it as all of Will's friends and family side-step around us.

Vyron pats my arm and feigns a smile and joins the other pallbearers in the front row. Punk Rock Freddie is up at the front, sharing stories with Will's parents, the three of them smiling with tears streaming down their cheeks. I sit on a pew in the back next to familiar faces. Rafael points out how everyone who comes in and dips their fingers in the holy water crosses themselves in my direction.

I say, "I guess they can see the devil in me."

He laughs, I don't.

Trenton says, "It should be Will sitting on this pew and any one of us in that casket." He shakes his head. "It's not fair, man. Will was a good person. One time, me and him was walking around the neighborhood, and this lady and her daughter were outside painting their house. They didn't know who the fuck we were. Will didn't even ask their names before he picked up a brush and started painting with them. All day long, he stayed, and he made me stay and help too, and we painted that whole fucking house. It was the middle of summer, hot as a motherfucker. Will wore that dumb leather jacket all day long. When we was finished, the lady who owned the house hugged us both and thanked us, asked if there was anything she could do. Will told her yeah.

He said, 'You got any coffee?'" Trenton sighs, slides down the pew until his head touches the back of it. "It should be one of us in that casket."

The back pew is silent for the rest of the service.

The funeral goes on for a couple hours. Will's sister gives the eulogy. Their parents weep. At least a dozen people go up to share memories. Will's nephew sings his uncle's favorite hymn. One of Will's cousins reads a poem she wrote. The priest says some shit about god having a plan that is beyond our comprehension and that Will touched a lot of lives in his short lifetime and though we may not understand it or like it, god is still using Will in his death.

Trenton bounces his elbows on his knees and holds his face in his intertwined hands, whispering curses to god. I touch his arm, say, "Send up a 'fuck you' from me while you're at it," and I walk out.

A 40 rolls out from under the seat when I pull up at my parents' house. I take a pull before I get out the car. Everyone else's vehicle is gone. Brandon is on the couch watching a B-list slasher on Netflix.

I say, "You home alone?"

He says, "Dad went back to work in New Braunfels. Mom and Serenity went to get their hair done. You going out tonight?"

I drop next to him on the couch. I say, "I don't feel like going anywhere tonight."

I take another pull from the 40. Tilt the bottle towards my thirteen-year-old brother. He shakes his head, says, "No, thank you."

I say, "You're so much different than I was at your age."

He says, "What'd you do today?"

"Just left a funeral. Friend of mine died."

"I'm sorry."

I shrug. "Happens."

On the movie, a woman is chainsawed in half. Gallons of bright red stage blood splash the walls.

Brandon says, "How old was he?"

I say, "Twenty-three."

"Damn."

"Yeah. He was a really good guy. Not like me." More chainsaws revving and women shrieking. I can't see what's happening anymore through the wet blur of tears. I tell Brandon, "He was more like you."

Brandon wraps his arms around my neck. I lay my head on his shoulder and take another pull.

CACTUS HONEY

My recording studio consists of a microphone with a pop filter, a keyboard, a bass guitar, and a laptop loaded with drum kits and sound FX and samples and shit like that. Also: a weight bench, a deer head, Christmas decorations, bicycles, and boxes of my stuff that need not be unpacked until I have a place of my own again. Yeah, my studio is otherwise known as my parents' shed.

My dad works out of town enough to warrant renting apartments or hotels on his employer's dime every time he gets moved around the state, each time further from home. He enjoys it, and I admire him for that, even if it's often from a distance. He's currently staying in New Braunfels, and that's where the rest of the family's gone to for the weekend. Along with putting together some new beats to rap over, the time alone presents the perfect opportunity to answer a question I recently brought up to myself: *wonder what it's like to smoke Adderall?*

After a trip to the corner store with the sign hanging over the broken gas pumps that reads I ASSURE YOU, WE'RE OPEN, I return to the shed with a glass rose tube to ease my curiosity.

I trash the rose and drop a few pills in the tube and burn a hole in the mic's pop filter from torching the bulb too close to it. Black smoke fills the glass and I blow it back into the pipe so as not to inhale the plastic coating off the capsules—just thinking about my health, you know. After the black melted shit cools, I torch the bulb again and inhale the grey clouds and hold for ten seconds.

My eyes roll back and sweat crowns my head. The high is more euphoria/less anxiety compared to eating or snorting the Addies. The taste is awful, like celery with a chemical burn.

I sink into my desk chair and minimize the music recording program and check my Facebook messages. One from my favorite indie book publisher asks for something I've written, so I guess I should start writing something, but first, I open a new tab and google "smoking Adderall" and find a drug forum post that suggests starting with a quarter chunk of a 20mg capsule, or one-twelfth the amount I just sucked into my lungs.

Perfect.

At least when the weekend is over and I've been awake for a three-day stretch and the tip of my tongue is where I feel my heart beating and I'm shivering in a corner, cradling myself and weeping with a sense of imminent doom, I'll know why.

I go into the house and brew dark roast coffee with chicory and pour it in a two-quart measuring cup and return to the shed for the next couple days. I write the entire time, focused as fuck thanks to the Addies. After a while, I stop paying attention to the pulsating walls. In the peak of the high, before the Doomsday comedown, I finish the story and send it to the publisher. Thirty thousand words of cannibal horror, anthropomorphic dinosaurs, a teenage nympho, and a man who gets high off honey he finds inside a cactus in the post-apocalyptic desert.

If it sees print, I'll dedicate it to the doctor who writes my amphetamine scripts.

SEASON

I'm inside a cabin in the woods and there's a half-naked blonde pounding on the door, screaming to be let in and rescued from the masked serial killer outside.

Just kidding.

I'm lying on my parents' couch either watching TV or staring at a blank screen when someone knocks frantic at the back door.

Brandon answers it and Sean almost knocks him over the way he side-steps inside, slamming the door behind him, and I already know he's tweaking. It's in the way he leans to the left and paces the room, and the way he scratches the skin off his arms in flakes—trying to get the bugs crawling under the surface out, and how he focuses on the curtains above the couch like he's counting the threads—dark-circled eyes all pupils behind his glasses. And it's in the way his behavior could be pantomiming me on most days.

Mom comes out of her bedroom and half walks/half sprints to the living room, that look on her face like she already knows who just walked in and that nothing is good about it.

Sean has his back to her. He's reaching to rustle Brandon's hair. Says, "When'd you get taller than everyone else?" He looks at me and says, "How'd you let this happen?"

"He did it all by himself."

Sean turns, sees Mom behind him and flinches, says, "Oh, shit." Laughs, hugs her. "How you doing?"

Mom hugs him back but keeps a locked jaw—she ain't taking no bullshit. "Why you flinching?" she says. "I ain't hit you yet."

Sean chuckles, says, "I was just coming over to say I love y'all, so, love you." He hugs Brandon. "Love you." Hugs me. "Love you." Opens the back door, says, "Y'all take care." Slams the door behind him.

Mom raises an eyebrow and her jaw drops to the side a little, that look that says *are you fucking kidding me?*

I follow her out the door after him, and we both see the red truck at the same time, both tell Brandon to stay inside.

Mom calls to Sean as he's opening the passenger side door and he stands behind it, puts his hands on his head and grins real big like he's being arrested in the middle of taking his kindergarten class picture.

"Where the hell do you think you're going?" Mom tilts her head at the driver. "Who's this?"

The driver leans across the seat, introduces himself with a handshake.

Mom says, "Hi, I'm sure you've heard of me. Don't fuck with my family. I'll kill you."

Says it all with a smile, too.

Sean puts his hands on her shoulders. That nervous grin. He says, "Calm down."

She says, "You think you're thug? I'll show you thug."

Sean laughs and pulls Mom's head to his chest, his arms engulfing her.

She says, "Please don't do this," and now she's crying in that trying-not-to kind of way.

Sean's friend digs his phone out, turns it sideways, tilts it this way and that.

Mom's speaking into Sean's chest, asking why. Telling him he's better than this.

Sean swipes a tear and flicks it away with his thumb. His hands are on Mom's shoulders again. He tells her not to worry and some other fuckery, probably promises something too.

Mom turns to me, eyes still on Sean, directing his attention. Forcing him to acknowledge who he's walking out on.

Sean's scratching again—the bugs have migrated into his neck—and he stares at the ground.

Mom says, "Just know I love you." Says it glaring. She storms back into the house.

My hands in my pockets. I toe a rock and then kick it. Look at Sean looking at the ground.

He says, "It's that season again."

"Yuh," I say, "it's that season. Try to keep your shit on the low, you know? Lot of local spots are hot. Couple friends of friends of mine got busted just last week—possession with intent."

Sean says, "Man, don't even worry 'bout that. I ain't gonna be anywhere around here."

"Where you going?"

"I can't say that," he says, "I'll check up on you, though. I'll see you again."

I say, "Yeah, sure. Through glass again?"

Sean runs a hand over his buzzed head and looks at the clouds, the gravel, something over his shoulder—anywhere but directly at me. "Fuck," he says. "Why you gotta say shit like that?"

I stare at him, dare him without saying anything to quit being a fucking pussy and look me in the eyes and tell me that yet again—when I need him most—he won't be there, that he'll never be there.

He throws his big arms around me and says, "Love you, brother," and I say it back, and he lets go before I can soak his shirt with my tears so he'd have to feel a part of me against him, making his flesh cold.

His smile has faded. Aside from the tattoos and crow's feet, Sean's face hasn't changed since he was eight and a half years old, holding my fragile new life in his hands. He gets in the truck and still won't look at me as his friend backs out and drives away, kicking dust. I walk out to the middle of the road and stand in his rearview and dare him again to look.

Mom's got these boxes and photo albums full of Kodak prints. I go backwards through the orange dates in the bottom right corners of the photos, skipping five—no, eight—no, ten years, knowing I have to go back farther than that, at least. When I've gone back eleven, twelve, thirteen years and still can't remember the last birthday Sean was there for, I give up.

21

I spend the first pre-dawn hours of my twenty-first birthday holding a gun to someone's head. The text conversation with Kim that led to this point started with the dick size of her ex-porn-star fuck buddy and ended in her asking favors. The last of it went like:

Kim—*So, my parents are out of town, putting down $ on the new house. I'm feeling horrible :(I think my ovary flipped again. I know it's the day before your b-day, but would you want to help me with the kids tonight? My parents will be back tomorrow. We can play video games!*

Me—*Yeah, I'll help with the kids. I want to see them more anyways before you move.*

Kim—*Thnx. Idk how I'm going to break it to Keith. The new place is like 8 hrs away.*

She's moving across the state with my kids, but yeah, poor Keith, the ex-porn star she randomly texted me about to say how many times she came when he fucked her in every position imaginable, the guy who would need Magnums if they used condoms.

I replied, *I'm sure he'll be lost without you.*

And I was being a smartass when I sent it, but now here he is, seeming pretty fucking lost—drunk and high and banging on the door I stand on the other side of, aiming a revolver.

Anjelica and Deandre are asleep upstairs. From where I stand, I can see Destiny sleeping in her swing in the living room. Kim's on the phone with 911, giving directions to the house for the ten millionth time.

I say, "Tell them they've got five more minutes—"

Kim holds a finger to her lips.

I move closer to the door with the gun. I say, "Tell them. I'ma put a bullet in this motherfucker."

She puts the phone against her shoulder, grabs my wrist as I'm reaching for the knob. There's a thud and a dragging sound as Keith slumps against the other side of the door and begins to cry, saying Kim's name over and over, saying, "Please let me in. We need to talk."

I say, "You open that door," I wave the revolver at Kim, "and I'ma blast anyone in front of it. I'll kill you and your boyfriend before I let that motherfucker up in here, threatening my kids. You realize that's what he's doing right now, right? Can you get that?"

"He said he wants to talk."

"He said when he texted you that he had a gun."

"I think that was a suicide thing."

"Him putting my kids in danger is a suicide thing, and so is defending him. So pick a side, bitch."

A voice is muffled against Kim's shoulder. She puts the phone to her ear, holds a finger up and mouths, *Wait.* Into the phone: "I'm sorry, what was that?" Kim runs over to a window, says, "Yes, I see the lights. They just pulled in. Thank you."

I wait until they take Keith's sobbing bitch ass to jail and be sure Kim presses charges before I put her stepdad's gun back in the safe.

I stay awake until the sun comes up, rocking Destiny in her swing. Anjelica and Deandre rush downstairs to tell me happy birthday. When Kim wakes up, I leave. I go to the corner store and set a bottle of Mad Dog on the counter and show my ID.

The clerk says, "Sorry, I'm not allowed to sell to you until eleven P.M."

I say, "Ain't that some shit." I put the Mad Dog back.

The clerk tells me happy birthday as I'm walking out empty handed and sober. I sit outside against the brick wall and smoke a cigarette. My phone vibrates. It's a text from my friend Antoine inviting me to a bonfire at his place. He doesn't know it's my birthday. I say, *I'll be there.*

A couple years ago, Antoine got fucked up on bath salts and he hasn't been the same since. He lives with his mom and her boyfriend in a trailer parked on a couple acres of dead grass and dirt. It's just him and Rafael mixing drinks on a foldout card table in the yard when I show up.

Rafael says, "What's up, homie. I didn't know you two knew each other."

Antoine whispers, "We go way back." He only ever whispers when he talks now. He says, "Thanks for coming. Sorry it's so lame."

I give Antoine a hug and say, "It's just what I needed, man. A couple good friends and some liquor."

"Well, shit, here you go." Antoine pours some vodka and some gin and some tequila and some red Kool-Aid in a Solo cup and hands it to me.

We drink hard like that all night.

Rafael sets his phone on the table and plays some beats he downloaded and we spit some bars. We climb the brush pile wielding gas cans and pour three gallons of gasoline on the brush and stand in the middle as Antoine strikes a match and counts to three and we all jump off at the same time when he drops it. We throw our fists in the air and howl at the flames. We sit by the fire and drink more.

Rafael gets that depressed kind of drunk where he's saying shit like: "When I was seven, my brother beat me up so bad I couldn't open my right eye for six months. I get by okay with contacts, but I'm still legally blind in this eye." He points at it. He says, "My dad is in prison and my mom is a fucking junkie. At least you have kids. I have nothing. I wish I had a kid." The flames are reflected in the water in his eyes, unblinking, getting closer to full blackout blindness. He says, "I'll probably kill myself tonight."

I say, "No, you won't."

"I might."

Antoine says, "Shut the fuck up. You're not killing yourself. And fuck your stupid family."

"You're right." Rafael toasts the fire. "Fuck them all." He tilts his drink back and kills it and hooks mine and Antoine's necks in the crooks of his elbows. He says, "You're good people."

We watch the embers spiral from the brush up into the trees and we pass out on the lawn waiting for a forest fire that never happens.

CYCLE

I torch a light bulb taped to a straw between my teeth.

I'm dripping sweat when it's so cold I can see my breath.

I tap out poems on the typewriter my parents bought me for Christmas, the first about taking a beating in a Catholic church back-alley that opens with the line *cut my tongue on the Virgin Mary's glass curves.*

I'm tweaking so hard my legs tell my brain to fuck off and move whenever they want, which is always when I'm trying to sleep.

I drive on a Friday to meet Kim in a convenience store parking lot, our halfway point for exchanging the kids. Thirty minutes into the return trip home, Anjelica pukes all over herself. I spend the next hour sweating on the side of the road, undressing her and holding her and stroking her hair until she stops whining. I use up all the baby wipes trying to clean the backseat. I imagine slitting Kim's throat

88

for giving the kids red Kool-Aid on an 82-degree day spent on the road.

My parents help in lining the kids up every few hours on Saturday for fever reducers. I rub their frail backs when they take turns throughout the night standing on a stool to reach the toilet.

I drive four hours back on Sunday to drop the kids off, the whole ride spent reaching behind my head rest to resume the kids' movie every time Deandre kicks the DVD player in a drawn-out tantrum being thrown because he wants to stay with me so bad he's willing to destroy his lungs and vocal cords, screaming how much he hates mommy and only loves daddy if it will make me turn around but it only makes me bite a hole in my lip trying to keep my own cries silent.

I eat glass.

Rafael kicks my ass at *Soul Calibur V.*

I grind my teeth.

Trenton kicks my ass at *Soul Calibur V.*

I sniff a line of snow white powder off a knife-scarred picnic table.

I KO every motherfucker on *Soul Calibur V.*

I lie on the floor like a fetus in the womb of a demon as people dance and drink and pop pills above me, my night owl pupils absorbing too much laser light/black light/strobe light, my heart rate synced up with the cymbals of a trap beat.

I could care less about *Soul Calibur V.*

I flush what looks like blood and coffee grounds down the toilet. Wipe my mouth on my sleeve. Crush some speed on the sink and sniff it up. That electricity—it shoots through my nostrils to my brain. I turn the lights off on the black-eyed skeleton in the mirror and return to whatever/whosever party this is, or I exit the corner store, or I lie back down on my great grandmother's couch and watch the kids play as my great grandmother comments on how well-behaved they are and how great of a job I'm doing.

I cop some dro from a guy who grows the shit in his closet and calls me 'brah' and sell it at twenty-five percent mark-up to a walking Polo ad in junior college so I can buy half a script worth of Addies from a med student and sell the ones I don't personally consume at three hundred percent mark-up to a trailer park full of meth heads.

I scan in, consolidate, and cut down a castle of boxes in a merchandise receiving room the size of a closet and think, *Fuck this job.*

I pull outdated pornography from the stand and tear the covers off to send back to the distributor and see the first page of every extreme bondage/senior citizen/morbidly obese/barely legal mag that the gross old men who buy or steal this shit decided to pass on.

I think, *No, seriously, this job can sit on a barbed wire dildo (as seen in a page one ad of* Maxxximum Perversum*)* and fuck itself raw.

I type a poem about breaking into the Houston Zoo at night and setting all of the tigers free.

I buy an eight ball of blow from the old hunchback car dealer and sell it to a work-from-home tattooist/beachside prostitute/mother of three I've known since back when she and I were both church kids. I drop enough dead presidents on the coffee table of a devil horn-tatted gun-toter named Angel to work out a two-for-one special on some thizz and devil dust and feel like Charlie with his golden ticket walking away with a baggy full of colored pills stamped with different symbols.

I dip my hand in the baggy and pop a purple yin yang.

I dip my hand in the baggy and pop a blue star.

I dip my hand in the baggy and pop a gold Superman.

I watch silhouettes grind and make out and throw stop motion punches at each other in front of a strobe light.

I spend a few thirsty days afraid to close my mouth because all of my teeth feel like they're ready to kamikaze out of my skull.

I pick the kids up.

Dad rents *The Lion King* DVD and per Deandre's requests, we watch it on triple repeat.

I drop the kids off.

I eat glass.

I rap over downloaded instrumentals in my parents' shed, plywood walls pulsing alongside the bass in my headphones.

I mix my own beats in the shed, an audience of shapeless shadow creatures with headlight eyes watching me cut/paste/drag highlighted blocks of instrument recordings across a computer screen until the sun comes up. No matter how much I blink or rub my eyes, the icons at the bottom of the screen won't stop jiggling.

I pick the kids up.

Mom and I take the kids to a waterpark and we're the only ones playing in the rain when it starts pouring from the still-bright, still-blue sky.

I drop the kids off.

I laugh at the concrete as it flies up at my face and I black out at the feet of friends who express concern with "oh, fuck" exclamations, hissed inhalations, and tilted heads before unanimous agreement that I'm fine and the spliff- and bottle-passing continues as the cold ground turns warm against my face.

I'm carried to a bare mattress that resembles a Pollack painting under a black light—pair of hands around each of my limbs, voices mumbling about dead weight.

I type a poem about being a fried strip of onion stuck between the teeth of a fair-weather friend.

I ball up all my typewriter poems while the ink's still wet and drop the ball in a handmade pit in the yard and light the poems on fire.

I breathe panic heavy with my face buried in the crook of my elbow.

I tell myself it'll be alright.

I'm such a liar.

IMMORTAL

I wake up to a dog tongue sliding across my forehead. Eric is in his boxers filling up a bong at the water cooler. He calls Nala back to the room with him and she licks my face again and runs off to get high.

This is one of those days I almost wake up with a smile. Then Anthony shouts "you motherfucker!" from the kitchen and chases me out with a charred cocaine-crusted saucepan and I limp around the corner of the house holding my hip.

I knock on Vyron's window and he opens it and I climb in and lie on my back on his bed. Vyron's eyes are dark and heavy. He's wearing a dress shirt, tie, and socks. He yawns and asks what time it is.

I check my phone for the time, ignoring the missed calls. "Ten past eight," I say. "You look like shit, by the way."

He rubs a fist in his eye socket and says, "Fuck me. I was supposed to be up two hours ago. You ain't got work today?"

"What day is it?"

"Tuesday."

"The fuck happened to Monday?"

"You went to work yesterday," Vyron says. "I remember 'cause you left the door open when you left and when I was leaving to go to work, there was a cat licking the mirror on the coffee table."

"That cat was probably flying," I say. "Anthony hit me with a saucepan."

Vyron chuckles and says, "The fuck he do that for?"

I tell him I ruined it cooking crack, how the first batch didn't turn out so well, and he says, "Since when do you cook crack?"

"Since last night," I say. "I copped some blow from a guy in Freeport, figured I could make a bigger profit off it if I turned it into rocks. So I googled 'how to cook crack' while everyone else was asleep."

I show him the baggy of yellow rocks. He opens it and sticks his nose inside and inhales deeply. Howls. Says, "Baby boy! You shoulda woke me up, I'da helped you."

"I tried. I shook you, but you didn't even move. You were hanging off the bed with one eye open and your pants around your ankles. Thought you were dead at first. I put my head on your chest to make sure your heart was beating."

"Shit." Vyron smiles, looks out the window. "I popped a Xannie last night."

"One Xanax did that to you?"

"I'm not used to pills the way you are." He punches me in the arm. "You heathenish muhfucka. You want to smoke some crack this morning?"

"Fuck that," I say, taking the baggy back and shoving it in my pocket. "I'm going to sell it."

"Give me ten percent," he says, "you can sell it all here, tonight. I'll invite every fiend and scumbag we know. It'll be a fucking rager."

We stand against a wall in the hallway and shout to hear each other.

"This enough people for you?" Vyron says.

"This is a fucking fire hazard," I say.

The toilet flushes behind the bathroom door and then the sink water runs and then a guy comes out scratching his throat. His eyes are glistening.

I touch Vyron's arm and tilt my head for him to follow. We lock ourselves in the bathroom and he rubs his hands together as I count the cash out on the sink and take ten per' off the top and fold the rest into my wallet.

"Baby boy!" Vyron rolls up his cut and stuffs the roll in his shoe.

We return to the party with grins on our faces.

Trenton and Rafael are huddled next to each other in a corner, shivering. They just ate an entire bag of shrooms.

I ask Rafael if he's still selling 'cid and he drops his car keys in my hand.

"Help yourself, bro," he says, teeth chattering. "In the glove box." He caresses my face and says, "You're beautiful."

I say, "Thanks, man."

I take a sheet of black acid from his glove box and hide it in Vyron's pillow case for later.

The Lloyd Kaufman film playing on the living room TV is on the scene where the fry cook begins mutating into a zombie chicken with a broomstick dick when Vyron claps a hand on my shoulder, panic in his eyes, and says, "Police at the door. He's asking for you."

I will myself into a more sober state as we round the corner, Vyron shoving people out of the way.

The cop stands on the front porch in the open doorway. He nods at me as we approach, and I focus on not glancing to the left so his eyes don't follow mine to the circle of crackheads smoking on the floor, or the powder on the coffee table. We step onto the porch with the cop and Vyron closes the door behind us.

The cop cocks his head back, giving the what's up.

I say, "Yes, sir?"

He says, "This your car, sir?" and points at my car parked parallel in the street.

"Yeah." My voice shakes. I clear my throat.

The cop walks as he talks. I'm trying to remember if I left any shit in the car as we follow him out to it. It doesn't catch up with me what the cop's saying until I see the egg yolk dripping down the driver door.

"Several cars on this block have been hit," the cop says. "It doesn't appear the egger has a preference."

Vyron puts a hand over his mouth and his shoulders bounce up and down.

"A serial egger?" I say, and Vyron can't control himself anymore. He screams a laugh that echoes down the dark street. I say, "Must be a slow night."

The cop smirks, says, "Yeah, it is. That's a good thing, though, when you do what I do." He points at the house—the wooden panels, roof shingles, and windows all vibrating from either the music or all the rapid heartbeats inside—and he says, "Celebrating something?"

Vyron says, "Just a little get together."

The cop looks sideways at Vyron. Opens his mouth to say something else.

There's the sound of an egg cracking against a windshield from up the street and we all turn in unison to see a shadowy figure in post-egg-throwing position beneath a street light. He looks at us looking at him and takes off running. The cop says something into the radio on his shoulder, thanks us/says goodnight, and chases after the serial egger.

Vyron fills a cup with warm water and helps me get the egg yolk that hasn't hardened yet off of my car.

* * *

Jermaine must have forgotten about me setting his arm on fire a few months ago, since I just spotted the golden canines in Jermaine's grin and locked eyes with him from across the room. My mind goes to the Glock I'd stolen from him, still hidden in the bushes next door. Before anything else, though, it's Vyron's open mic freestyle that has everyone crowded into the sun room, and it's my turn with the mic. On his laptop, Vyron selects a trap beat he produced, and through the loudspeaker set up in the corner, a synthesized classical violin is joined by rapid-fire hi-hats and then a bass line that reverberates down the block, rattling windows and setting off a few car alarms.

I lose myself in the circle of bodies. The tracers following their every move— that's the ecstasy in my system. My tongue moving too fast for my brain to keep up—or maybe vice versa—that's the speed. I spit some bars in aggressive tongues.

If karma is a bitch, tell her go fuck herself/The worst shit that could happen, I can do to myself/My daughter's photo and my drugs are stashed on the same shelf/[gibberish]/Run ya pockets, don't play, bitch, I don't do this shit for fun/This candy ain't for children, ain't no safety on this gun/[gibberish]/Name on my birth papers shoulda read "Legion"/When my moms pushed me out, she exorcised a demon/[gibberish]/Chips on my shoulder serve the devil's luncheon/Dine on lithium just to function/

Spine's been sawed on since I's a munchkin/[gibberish]/To every muthafucka who scribes my name on a bullet/If your trigger finger's nervous, I'll be happy to pull it

I put my index and middle finger against my temple/ bend my thumb forward/close my eyes and fall back against Vyron, handing him the mic as he catches me and shoves me off and everyone cheers at my mimed suicide.

I sink into the sea of people and feel the music move through me, changing the way my heart beats. Vyron raps in what he calls a string of pearls lyrical arrangement, each line referencing or spinning off the one that came before it. He freestyles about hacking the heads off the neighbor kids and rolling and having an arsenal of automatic weapons in his trunk and it's pure poetic genius.

He leaves his laptop open with the mic next to it and says anyone's free to fuck with it, then he follows me to the kitchen and we make our own cocktails, which for us consists of pouring liquor into a glass then sprinkling some drug in powder form into it. For Vyron, it's strawberry Ciroc and Molly. I open the cabinet under the sink and reach behind the bleach and peroxide and pull out a bottle with a tentacled creature on the label—"unleash the Kraken!"— and fill a plastic cup, then crush an amphetamine tablet on the counter and stir in the blue powder.

I bring the cup to my lips with my eyes closed, take a sip. Set it down on the counter next to where Jermaine leans in on his elbows and grins.

His breath smells sour when he says, "Hey, bruh, how 'bout we let bygones be what they are?"

The impulsive urge to grab the top of his head and slam his face into the counter—that's the speed. The too-high-to-care pacifism blocking said impulse—that's the ecstasy.

I shrug and say, "Sure."

From behind me, Vyron says, "Don't start shit, won't be shit."

Jermaine says, "Speaking of shit," and buries his hand up to the forearm in his pocket, feels around a couple seconds, staring at the ceiling as he does, feeling the texture and size of what's in there to find the right shit: a rock in shoddy plastic wrapping that eclipses Jermaine's right eye when he digs it out and holds it up between his forefinger and thumb and says, grinning, "A gift." He holds it out in his palm under my chin. "For you, bruh."

We look each other in the eyes for a few seconds, studying. He's smiling, I'm not—not until I take another look at the rock in his hand. Its jagged shape, its milk-stained glass clarity.

I take and pocket the crystal and say, "Thanks."

Jermaine holds his hands palms up at his sides/tilts his head/shows his gold canines. "I take care of my friends."

I fake a smile and say, "I have to take a piss." I weave through people drinking/rolling/popping/smoking/laughing/rapping/talking/spazzing/making out/staring at their hands, cross the backyard, jump the fence, and grab the Glock 9 from the bushes next door, exactly where I left it.

I check the clip and tuck the hammer in the front of my jeans and jump back over the fence and join a small group hanging out on the back porch. Vyron runs out of the house and grabs Trenton, whose lips are separating for an incoming spliff, and sticks his tongue in Trenton's mouth. Trenton smiles and rubs Vyron's cheek and says, "Thanks, bro," and takes a drag on the spliff.

Vyron throws his arms in the air, spins, grabs me by the shoulders. He puts his face so close to mine, I can count the pink lines around his irises and smell the chemical sweetness seeping from his pores. Instead of kissing me, though, he says, "Stay away from the Kraken." Then he laughs and runs back in the house.

I laugh, too, even though I don't get the joke until later, when I'm doubled over with my head in the toilet vomiting Kraken and what Vyron discovers was rat poison after knocking out one of Jermaine's golden canines, along with some other teeth.

Vyron drags Jermaine's face across the sidewalk and picks him up and body slams him on the hood of his car, says, "You step up in this house or go near baby boy again, I'ma kill you." Then he slaps him in the face for good measure and comes back to pick me up by the armpits and carry me to his bed.

I ask Vyron if he killed Jermaine, and he says no, and tells me what he did do.

I say, "Fuck that punk bitch." I curl into the fetal position and say, "Ow, my stomach."

Vyron says, "Get some rest, you'll be a'ight."

I ask him to turn off the light before he leaves the room. I wish I hadn't, but it hurts too much to holler.

I reach inside the pillow case for the sheet of acid and put a window pane on my tongue and keep my eyes open.

The room spins into a thick vortex of black ink.

My mind starts going to that place and I pull the Glock out of my pants and hold it. Feel its weight, its cold touch. I stick the barrel in my mouth, stretching my lips so far apart the commissures tear and bleed down to my chin. The barrel touches the inner walls of my cheeks. I pull the gun out of my mouth and exhale. I put the gun against my temple, finger touching the trigger—but just touching.

That coldness.

At some point, I either get up and turn the light on or I become nocturnal, and I stare at the wall.

Anthropomorphic mushrooms jump out of a velvet poster and square dance in the middle of the floor.

The edge of the bed stretches to touch the wall at the other side of the room and I feel six inches tall.

The cartoon fawn in the Disney movie poster gives me a menacing look and grows sharp teeth and antlers. I remember the gun in my hand. Aim it between the fawn's big blue eyes. I fire twice, and the fawn is just a curious big-eyed fawn again, sniffing flowers. Two bullet holes in its head.

Vyron rushes into the room and extends a hand that could close around my entire body and crush me, but instead he just takes the gun away. A volcano is growing up from his chest. Lava and smoke where his head should be.

I feel normal size in his arms when Vyron carries me out to his car, lays me down across the backseat.

He drives for what feels like hours and I forget we're not in a boat when the waves start crashing against us.

Somehow, Vyron drives us safely to dry land. He pulls me out by the legs and puts his shoulder under my armpit and we walk this way down a wooded trail, past the sign that reads *walking trail closed dusk to dawn*, and we sit at the edge of a cliff overlooking the river, my head against his neck. I tell him I think I'm dying.

"You're not dying," Vyron says. "You're going to live forever."

I close my eyes.

We wake up at the edge of the cliff, squinting at the rising sun. We brace our hands on the huge roots of a tree and pull ourselves up. Brush the dirt off.

Vyron says, "You okay?"

He doesn't look like the one to be asking that question.

I nod my head yes.

We use each other for balance walking back to the car.

"You can get some more sleep in my bed," he says.

I shake my head. "Gotta go to work."

"You going to be a'ight today?"

"I'm going to live forever."

Between the park and Vyron's house, I drift in and out of sleep, the window warm against my temple.

I brush my teeth and sniff a crushed Adderall off the sink and go to work.

KORIN, PT. 1

I work with the most beautiful woman in the world, but she's only there for an hour and a half on mornings when we scan inventory before she leaves to go to her regular job in the environmental department at the County building.

I want to tell her I think she's the most beautiful woman in the world.

I have no fucking clue how to talk to the most beautiful woman in the world.

So one day, in front of her, I tell Nicki—the chick who works full-time with me in the back room—I tell her, "Korin is going to have my love child."

This becomes a running joke. I'm not sure Korin appreciates it.

I hate how fucking awkward I am sometimes.

One day, we're doing video inventory, and the last fixtures to scan are in the foyer between two sets of double doors leading outside. Korin has started on one already. I punch the fixture number in my gun and start scanning next to her before anyone else can.

We don't say much, maybe hello.

There's the echoing beeps of our guns scanning barcodes.

Korin finishes her fixture first and walks out of the foyer and I hear a click between the double doors, look up to see her standing behind the glass. She tilts her head and smirks and gives me the finger.

All I can do is smile back.

She's the most gorgeous person I've ever seen.

If she smiled and flipped me off every morning for the rest of my life, I'd die happy.

TROUBLE

My mom stands in the doorway, biting her lip, watching me exchange the clothes in my backpack for clean ones. She says, "I wish you wouldn't do this."

I say, "Do what? We're just going to hang out."

"Where?"

"I don't know. I don't care. We'll see where the night takes us."

She follows me out to the truck Sean left in the last time he stopped by. I throw my backpack behind the bench seat and Sean introduces me to his friend, DJ or MC or LP—some two-letter musical acronym for a name I immediately forget. My mom gives Sean the third degree and he says, "We're just hanging out, don't worry."

It doesn't take. She calls before we get to the end of the road, pleading with me to come back. "I have a bad feeling," she says, "I need you to trust me. My chest is hurting over this. You do not need to go anywhere tonight."

"I'll be fine, Mom," I say. "I can handle myself."

I hang up. Sean gives me a couple XOs and a Coke to wash them down with.

We stop at the corner store with the broken pumps and Sean tells what's-his-face to pop the hood and pretend to work on the engine or something. We sit for a minute. A white Acura pulls up and Sean gets out to talk to the guy in the passenger seat. He says, "How much for five?" and the guy says, "How much you got?" and Sean slides a roll of cash over the window, checking his shoulder, and the guy hands him three bags rubber banded together. Sean asks the guy if he knows of any action going on tonight. Guy says he'll let him know. Sean says, "A'ight, I'll see you."

What's-his-face closes the hood and we drive to a different gas station, one where the pumps work, 'cause the tank's on empty. Sean says, "I'm broke now. Y'all got cash?"

What's-his-face says he has five dollars. I put twenty in the pot.

Sean says, "This is enough to get us to the beach, huh? Fill up, we'll go in and pay."

As we're walking inside, Sean says, "You know how to fight, right?"

I say, "I can hold my own. Why?"

"In case shit goes down tonight. I want to know that you can take care of yourself. If you can't, get somewhere and duck. You know how to shoot a gun, right?"

"The fuck's going down tonight?"

Sean smiles. He pays the clerk. "I didn't say anything was going down tonight. I said, 'if.' All I'm for sure about tonight is we're going to get fucking high, and fucking drunk, and we're going to fuck some fine ass women."

I say, "I can hold my own. Don't worry about me."

Sean says, "I'll always worry about you, brother. If anything, just holler, and I'll be there—locked and loaded."

We drive towards the beach. Sean says, "One day, I'ma have a fuckload of money. I'm talking stacks on stacks on stacks. And I'ma buy a big piece of land and build houses all over that motherfucker so any family or friends that want to live there, can. But I'ma tell them, 'There's guns and drugs and some thug-ass shit that goes down around here, anyone that doesn't like that is free to get the fuck out.'"

My dad calls and Sean keeps on with his Tony Montana-sized fantasy and I tell him to shut up so I can hear my dad talk.

There's something different in his voice, but not unfamiliar.

"Please," he says, desperate. "Just trust me for tonight, please come back home."

I hang up. I'm not happy about it, but I tell Sean to turn around.

"The fuck you mean?" he says.

"I mean take me back, damn it."

"They're just tripping."

"I know," I say. "I'd rather not worry them, though. I'll hit you up soon. Just take me back tonight."

Sean tells what's-his-face to turn around and take me home.

They drop me off and burn out.

My parents meet me in the driveway. They say, "Thank you." Relief in their eyes.

I say, "I'll be in the shed."

I stay up all night, channeling my frustrations into a microphone.

I know Sean gets trashed, 'cause it's four days before I hear from him again.

THE GODDAMN DEVIL

I've been fighting with my parents a lot lately—over everything, over nothing.

One day, I decide I can't stand it anymore and storm out in the middle of a heated argument over how I'm living or not living or whatever, and I slam the kitchen door shut behind me and it's not two seconds later my dad's got a grip on my arm and spins me to face him and we both look at each other like we're waiting for the other to throw the first punch, but instead of swinging his fist, my dad yells some stuff about my shitty attitude and disrespect towards my mom. He yells until his face turns red and I can feel my chest caving in and my eyes starting to water.

He stops yelling. Eyes shaking: that *say something* look.

I say nothing, just glare at him: that *I hate you* look, but it's not towards him—more like, the parts of myself that came from him. I wish I could say *sorry you ended up with me as a son,* but since I'm too much like the man, I walk away with my jaw clenched and get in my car and drive away.

Another time, it's something like four in the morning, and I'm yelling to the point the neighbors have turned their porch lights on and I can feel their eyes through the blinds burning holes in the back of my neck.

But my mom and I, we're not fighting.

I'm just—I don't know, I'm higher than fuck. Haven't slept in a while. I'm fed up with this life to the point my only shred of hope is the next one will be better and I'm leaning again towards speeding up that process. I say that last part out loud and my mom holds her hands at her sides, palms up. She shrugs defeated.

She says, "Why do you think that way?"

I tell her the truth. "I don't know." I put a finger on my temple. "It's like I have a monster clawing around inside my head, pulling on stuff, whispering into my subconscious. Like I'm possessed, kinda, but not. I'm controlling myself, I'm always me, but that's the problem. I'm fucked up. I'm worse than the goddamn devil."

Tears pooling in her eyes. "You don't know how much that kills me," she says, "every time you say that." Crying so hard she has to force the words out: "I'm your mother, and I know I can't do anything for you, and that kills me."

I've stopped shouting, backed against a tree for balance. I shrug, shake my head. "I'm sorry." Everything turns into a blur through the tears. I say, "I'm sorry I'm your son."

She wraps her arms around me. Streams run down my neck and back. She says, "Don't fucking say that. You don't ever have to be sorry for that. I love you. I just want to help you. I would do anything. Just tell me what I could do to help you."

I think on it for a long time, really trying, wanting so badly for the sake of us both to have an answer.

I hug my mom tight, trying to offer some comfort, soften the blow. I say, "I can't think of anything."

SELF-PORTRAIT

My phone buzzes under my head at five in the morning. Brandon is asleep in the bed above me, so I hit a button on the phone before Waka Flocka Flame starts yelling about being on that fuck shit. I meant to hit the red one.

It's a banshee on the other end, then a hand-over-mouth smack that muffles the screaming.

I check the caller ID, put the phone against my ear and whisper. "Syd?"

Deep, shaky breathing. If she wasn't tripping, I'd assume she was either being stabbed to death or masturbating.

I ask Syd if she understands that window panes are not gummy bears.

"I'm inside the television," she says. "But I don't want to be a rotating gem display. Come change the channel. Make me an ultraviolent cartoon again."

I say, "Don't you got a boyfriend to drop acid with?"

She says, "I am static," then mimics an old TV with no signal.

114

"You have any left?"

She growls. "Do you know where your children are?!"

I hang up.

I call work and leave a message in my best sick voice that I can't make it in today.

I drive to Syd's place and find the sliding glass patio door is cracked open and I let myself in.

The bottom floor of Syd's town house is a gallery of abstract expressionist paintings. Easel trays filled with a diverse range of mediums: bleeding spray paint cans, shriveled tubes of toothpaste, a half-empty jar of pesto, a dry blood-crusted razor.

Syd sits cross-legged in the glow of her television, staring at a blue screen and mimicking the piano from the *Cheers* theme song.

Today, Syd's mohawk is every color spray paint in her possession. Her head has a chemical potency.

I go upstairs to her bedroom and find the sheet of acid on her nightstand, a couple window panes left. I chew on one and lie on her bed and stare at the ceiling, looking for characters in the texture. In the corner above the door, a bunny devours the tail of a freaked-out water dragon as the devil watches in doubled-over hysterics.

The Lucy hasn't even hit me yet.

When it does hit, my vision goes kaleidoscope. I put my hands in front of my face and a hundred fingertips collide. Time does not exist. For a moment or for a lifetime, I stare at my hands. I've reached the pinnacle of enlightenment. I know everything. I am everything. I'm inside of myself and I am another person, another creature, a black monster. I crawl outside of myself, outside of the kaleidoscope world and into one where everything is a different shade of grey, then I crawl down the stairs.

Syd is swimming around on the carpet, cheeks ballooned. I crawl across her imagined water to the legs of an easel and remember how to use my legs to stand up.

I grab fistfuls of acrylic tubes—black, white, charcoal, mercury, some in-between greys—and squeeze them until they burst. I paint with my fingers on the walls of Syd's town house. Crude skulls/warped faces/optic nerve-tailed eyeballs.

In front of the bathroom mirror, I paint my face every shade of grey and I smile, content with myself, and it's like that for the rest of my life until I die and my skin rots, my bones deteriorate, and the last thing to fade is my smile, and then the world is in color again, my face is green and pink and purple and blue and without smile, and Syd stands at the bathroom door with her hands on her head, fingers digging into her skull, her teeth clenched.

She says, "Get the fuck out," so I get the fuck out, throwing a hand up to shield my eyes from the sun.

I get in my car and drive until I hit Surfside. I wash my face in the ocean and watch streaks of color roll out on the tide.

EROSION

The inside of my stomach is a crimson pool of coagulated blood. I know this 'cause I'm watching the coffee ground vomitus (that's a technical term, I think) swirl down the toilet. Broken glass and razor blades parade march through my intestines.

At work, I can't even stand. I leave early because the act of scanning barcodes on t-shirts and re-folding them is too strenuous.

I can't hold anything down. I stare with intimidated fear at a bowl of chicken noodle, imagine the soup as wet cement. I shovel it in my mouth 'cause it's good for me—I need the nutrients, right, Mom?–and it's like concrete when it goes down, just the same when it comes back up.

* * *

My mom drives me to the doctor who writes my Adderall scripts. A nurse weighs me in at ninety-five pounds and her face goes red. She runs down her checklist of questions as fast as she can, averts her eyes when I catch her looking. I wonder if I really look so terrible that strangers think it's rude or bad luck to make eye contact with me. Decide yeah, I probably do.

The doctor comes in, listens to me for a couple minutes, says I should see a different doctor.

This other doctor specializes in gastrointestinal problems. He asks me to lie flat on my back and sit straight up. It takes me a minute of cringing and picturing a crosscut saw in my abdomen.

The doctor says, "Sitting up causes you that much pain?"

I nod, catching my breath.

Doc looks at his clipboard, then back at me. He says, "And you don't do any recreational drugs?"

I shake my head no.

He says, "Are you sure?"

I glance over at my mom sitting in the corner of the room.

Doc nods. "I want to schedule an endoscopy."

"What's that?"

"It's where I put a camera down your throat to look

around in your stomach. You'll have to be put under."

I lean back against the wall while my mom gets the surgery date from the front desk and the doctor catches me in the hall with a book about finding peace in Jesus.

He says, "I recommend reading this as well."

On our way out, I give the book to my mom. "The doctor wanted you to have this," I say.

Days filled with blood tests and frigid, white-walled rooms.

Blood swirls from my arm into a vial and everything fades to black. When I come to, my mom's in the room, and she and the phlebotomist are all panicky.

This is how we find out I do not have AIDS, but I am hypoglycemic.

They say I'm severely dehydrated, need a drip. They can never find my veins. They keep stabbing and pulling out and rubbing their chins/scratching their heads and passing the IV needle off to a different nurse.

They say to each other, "Here, you try."

I say, "Can I try?"

Some of them consider it, but they all say no, wishing they could say yes. I keep swearing my veins are there, somewhere, I think.

They say, "Are you sure?"

* * *

Before they roll me into the operating room, I say, "I don't want to be here."

Mom says, "What would you rather do?"

"Die."

"That's not an option."

Fluids rush through my veins. Fluorescents stab my eyes. I'm freezing under a pile of heated blankets. I say, "It feels like an option."

A nurse rolls me back to the OR, where I'm hooked and strapped to more beeping machines.

The anesthesiologist puts a mask over my face, says, "Count backwards from eleven."

On five, one of the machines drones and Doc looks at me, jaw slacking. I flick my chin up in question before blinking out, and he says, "You shouldn't be alive right now."

Thanks for the honesty, Doc.

I feel the best I have in a while the second time I die.

The world welcomes me back with pictures of my insides. Doc is pointing out the infected erosions while my vision's still blurring into focus. It's going to take some expensive drugs with zero mind-altering effects to repair the lining in my stomach.

My mom says, "Your dad should be here any minute."

"So fast?" I say.

"I told him how bad you were. He jumped in his truck before hanging up with me."

When it all comes back to me, I tell my parents about dying on the table.

My dad's eyes go wide.

My mom is livid. She says, "I'm writing a letter."

None of the surgery bills get paid.

I wash the expensive stomach pills down with whiskey.

I go back to work.

KORIN, PT. 2

I pick a clean shirt, one with buttons.

Serenity catches me with the bathroom door open, checking myself in the mirror. She says, "I've never seen you give this much of a fuck before."

I'm not sure of my own intentions tonight. I don't expect Korin will want to be more than friends, and she's not the type to be a quick lay. Outside of our small talk and joking around to inject a little life into mundane early mornings at work together, I don't know her at all. I know she works three jobs and has a beautiful smile and she dresses nice and possesses a perfect balance of snark and class. I know she's gorgeous. I know enough to know she's too good for me.

Still.

She makes me want to open every door for her.

I have to turn on Sixth Ave to get to Korin's house, which is a block away from Vyron's place. It's my first time driving down this road sober. I want to have a clear head on our first date. I'm not a fan of the nerves that go along with that.

We have dinner at a local café. She orders a salad with a water and I order quesadillas or something with a long island iced tea. I ask what's with the salad, and she says the County Clerk's Office has this annual fitness challenge and she's determined to win it.

With a body like hers, I think she has an unfair advantage. I tell her this in so many words that aren't as slick.

She says, "I like a challenge."

We talk about our families, about how she took care of her mom in her last days and now her dad and brother are all she claims. "The rest of my family are pieces of shit," she says.

I say, "I get that." I tell her about Sean, about how he's my third cousin by blood but my grandparents adopted him, so he's legally my uncle, but we grew up together and we're real close so we claim each other as brothers. "Brothers is what we're like," I say, "so brothers is what we are."

She says, "I get that."

Something about her makes me transparent. Before I kill my drink, I mention a little bit about my drug abuse, and that I told my mom I was worse than the goddamn devil, which is exactly what I would think of my son if I was my mother. Korin doesn't flinch at any of this. She has a candid aura that makes me want to cut open my chest and be open and vulnerable.

I'm still not sure of my intentions, but at the end of the first date, I'm more hopeful about the possibility of an "us"—not because of anything I did or said, but because I barely know her and already want to spend the rest of eternity knowing her better.

It's the second time we go to the movies—third date—before I work up enough nerve to hold her hand. I don't know what it is about going a single night with no illicit consumption that makes me feel so goddamn anxious, but it doesn't make me want to rush to the men's room and eat some glass. It just makes me that much happier when we finally touch each other on that ground level of intimacy.

She invites me in to drink wine and talk on the couch.

It's three A.M. before either of us realizes.

I linger between the threshold and the concrete on my way out, and she kind of sways in the doorway, biting a corner of her lip.

We read it in each other's eyes.

Her kiss is electric.

BACKSEAT

Mom and Serenity are screaming at each other about something. I really don't want to be here, or anywhere for that matter.

I think I let someone know that I'm going out, won't be back, but maybe I just walk out to my car and drive to a gas station and buy a po'boy wrapped in plastic and eat it in the parking lot of the entertainment store where I'm supposed to be clocking in six hours from now. I sit on the asphalt and lean against the front tire and smoke a cigarette. Light another. I text Korin. I mention I'm not happy at home, but not that I'm sleeping in my car. Eventually, we say goodnight. I put my iPod on shuffle and crawl into the backseat and fall asleep.

Couple hours later, a flashlight shines on my face through the window. I'm out of the car and showing my driver's license before I fully wake up. I tell the cop this is where I work and he asks if it's also where I live and I shake my head.

I say, "Just didn't want to be at home tonight."

The cop says, "You ain't got friends to stay with? Other family?"

"Didn't want to bother anyone. My shift starts in just a few hours anyways, so—" I shrug.

The cop nods, looks off in the distance, remembering something. He says, "If I call up here in a few hours—"

I say, "You'll hear my voice on the other end."

He hands my license back, points in my backseat. "Those fold down?"

"Yeah."

"Might be more comfortable."

"Yeah."

The cop watches me fold the seats down and leans in to look around the inside of my car. "What's in the backpack?"

"Clothes."

The cop nods. "You have a good night."

He gets in his squad car and drives away and I crawl in the backseat and lock the doors and use my backpack as a pillow, glad for once to not have any drugs on me.

GOOD SHIT

I pull up to a corner store near Freeport where Sean is waiting in someone else's truck and I follow him the rest of the way to this guy Marshall's house. When we pull into the driveway, he and his wife are smoking cigarettes on the porch. Sean and I lean against the brick and light up.

"You remember my little brother."

Marshall says, "Been a minute."

We touch fists.

"This is my wife, Veronica."

Veronica says, "What's up."

I slap Sean's arm and nod at the driveway. "So what happened to your truck?"

"Oh. Yeah, man, Lexi kinda beat the shit out of it with a bat. We got in a little fight, so I ducked down here for a bit. Friend of mine loaned me the truck. I don't think it's hot. Best I'm not driving my own truck right now anyways. I got people after me."

Veronica chuckles. She says, "Every time I see you, you're saying you got people after you."

Sean says, "I ain't ever lying. It ain't even good to know my name around these motherfuckers. I got a homie was getting a haircut, said a group of about ten dudes came up in the barber shop with a metal bat asking where I was. He told them they could fuck themselves and they beat the living shit out of him in front of his son. Beat the barber up and smashed the windows too. My homie called and told me this from the hospital."

Marshall says, "And you're staying at my fucking house?"

Sean smiles. "Chill, bro. This was up in Wharton. Don't nobody know where I am, what I'm driving, or who I'm with. It's all good."

Veronica says, "Jesus. What the fuck did you do this time?"

Sean shrugs and says he doesn't remember and we all have a good laugh about it.

Veronica shakes her head, flicks the butt of her cigarette into the yard. She says, "We need more cigarettes."

Marshall says, "A'ight." To me and Sean, he says, "Want to come with?"

Sean slaps my arm, says, "Let's take your car, since your crazy-ass parking blocked the damn driveway."

"You don't like my driving," I toss him the keys, "be my guest."

Sean leans the seat way back. Rolls the windows down. He waves at a passing cop and the cop waves back. He turns the stereo up. "What you listening to?"

"Instrumental shit," I say.

To the backseat, he says, "Yo, Marshall, you gotta hear my little brother freestyle."

Marshall says, "You freestyle?"

I say, "Not really. I'd rather write my lyrics."

Sean says, "He's lying. He can spit fire." He hits the skip back button and the track starts over. He says, "Give us some bars." He pulls into the corner store parking lot.

I say, "We're already here."

Sean locks the doors. "We ain't in a rush."

I sigh. "Fine." I feel out the beat a little bit, then let loose. *Scribing the book of life with a blood-tipped pen/Each line I write is two breathed in, so the spine stays slim/Only a year past twenty, but I'm close to the end/Live like a master of Zen, but still a bastard of sin/I'll be the trillest muthafucka 'til the credits read "fin"/Subliminal criminal, keep the chatter on minimal/ Break ya neck looking up to me, where I sit is the pinnacle/I'll make Blanco look pitiful and turn El Chapo cynical/Fuck these OGs, they just old gangstas, I'm the original*

Sean says, "I know you got more than that."

I say, "Nah, that's it. I'll start saying stupid shit if I go too long."

Marshall says, "That was dope."

I say, "Thanks."

129

* * *

When we get back to Marshall's place, he reaches under the couch and pulls out a Winchester box full of weed. Puts his face in it. "This shit smells like heaven."

He tosses me three bags, calling out their names as he does: Blue Dream, Grape Ape, Black Cherry Soda. "That's some top-shelf hybrid shit right there."

I sniff one and say, "This one smells like blueberry."

He says, "You want to try that one?"

I say, "Sure," and toss him the bag.

"Keep the other two. Sean told me what you do for a living. I want fifteen a gram, so you can split it up how you want, mark it up however—but do the math, I want fifteen per gram."

I glare at Sean and he grins at me. He says, "You got any pills on you?"

Marshall says, "What kind of pills?" His eyes go wide and he stops packing the bowl for a second when I set the speed on the coffee table. He looks around the room and drops his tone to a whisper. To Sean: "Where's Veronica?"

Sean leans back in the easy chair, looks down the hall. He says, "I think I hear the shower."

Marshall nods at the speed. "Want to trade?"

I say, "No."

"Sell it to me, then."

Sean looks back and forth between us.

"Look, I won't sell it," Marshall says. "I don't know shit about pills. I just want to try it for myself. How much for two?"

"Sixty," I say.

He pulls three twenties from a roll of bills and I give him the speed and he pops one with a water and puts the other in his pocket.

Sean cocks his head down the hall and I grab the speed and follow close behind him.

Marshall says, "I'm still packing this bowl."

Sean says, "We'll just be a minute."

We pass Veronica coming out of the bedroom, toweling her hair. "Marshall packing a bowl?" she says.

Sean nods and watches her walk to the living room. He grunts and says, "She is so fucking fine." He closes the door behind us in the guest bedroom, where his suitcase is open on the floor and his clothes are scattered all over the furniture. "A'ight," he says, "give me the speed."

I hand him the orange bottle and he tips a pill out on the dresser. Crushes it under a dollar bill with his fist. "Let me see your debit card," he says, and I oblige, and he cuts a line for each of us. "That enough?"

I tip another pill out. "Cut that and it will be."

Sean laughs. He says, "You can have that. I'll stick to half." He rolls the dollar and sniffs the half-line up through it and blinks a few times. Says, "Oh, yeah."

131

I rail the other line on the dresser and crush the second tablet and put my face in the powder.

Sean says, "It's probably not right, us doing drugs together."

I say, "I'd do them without you."

"Yeah. Fuck it."

We return to the living room. Marshall and Veronica have already started on the bowl. I hit it once for a taste, then pass. I don't want it to kill my buzz.

Marshall says, "That's some good shit, huh?"

"Yeah," I say. "Very smooth."

In the time it takes to cash the bowl, Sean holds up the circle at least three times, smoking it like he's the only one in the room. He stares at the television. Some game show. He glances over and sees me texting, says, "You got a girl now, huh?"

"Yeah," I say. "She's amazing."

Veronica says, "Aww."

"He's in love with her," Sean says, sinking further into the easy chair. "He told me."

"I did not tell you that."

"You might as well have."

The room is thick with berry-scented smoke.

Marshall says, "Sean, you high?"

Sean says, "No shit, I'm fucking high." He wipes drool off the corner of his mouth.

It's too low-key in here for the high I'm feeling. I step

out in the backyard and toss a stick around with Marshall's pit bull. The fourth time he brings it back, he wants to play tug and nearly yanks my arm out of socket. I say, "You're a beast." I find a can of black spray paint in the garage and tag the word *beast* on his dog house.

The sun sets. A game of dominoes is going down in the kitchen. A lanky guy in chemical plant garb who's a few front teeth short of a full smile lets himself in the front door and Marshall almost knocks over the table when he springs up.

"Oh, it's only this motherfucker," he says, sitting back down. "The fuck did you do to your hair?"

The lanky guy pulls a chair up between me and Sean and sits in it backwards. He touches the black- and blonde-striped mohawk on his head. "The mohawk is coming back, man," he says. "I think it's punk rock."

Sean says, "You look like a goofy-ass skunk."

"Fuck you."

Sean introduces me and the skunk. He says, "This is your third cousin or something like that. You two are probably closer in blood than we are."

Up until now, Sean has always introduced us as brothers. Genealogy be damned, brothers is what we've been. Maybe I'm dwelling too much on it, but for the rest of the night, I'm pretty bummed out.

I text Korin and realize where I'd much rather be.

* * *

After cutting the hybrid dope down into several nickel bags and stuffing it under the carpet in my trunk, it only takes a few phone calls and parking lot rendezvous to rid myself of it. Good shit sells itself.

KORIN, PT. 3

Soon as I take the turn on Sixth Ave, it's red and blues flashing in the rearview.

I noticed the cruiser creeping up on me at the lost stop sign. Sat there for a long time on purpose with no traffic. So as I'm pulling over into a church parking lot, window rolled down and license ready, I really have no idea what's going on.

The cop says, "Do you know why I'm pulling you over this evening?"

I say, "I have no idea."

"You ran that stop sign back there."

"Well, yeah, after I stopped at it for a minute."

He snickers. "Why your eyes so big, man? You on anything?"

"My eyes are big?"

"And your hands are kinda—" He holds his hand up, flat, makes it shiver. "You nervous?"

I say, "A little."

"Why you nervous?"

"You're wearing a badge, aren't you?"

"Sir, would you be willing to let me search your vehicle?"

"Sure. But why?"

"You're acting a little strange, very jittery. I want to search it for drugs."

"I don't have any, so go ahead."

We go through the routine. I step out and he pats me down. Of course he finds the Adderall. I let him know I have a script for that, for my severe ADD.

He says, "Where were you heading tonight?"

Were. Like I'm already convicted. Like, wherever it was, it's not where you're going anymore.

I say, "My girlfriend's house to pick her up. We were going to get ice cream, 'cause she's been on this fitness challenge at work, and now it's over and we were going to celebrate."

He says, "That sounds nice. Now, if I search your car, is there anything you want to go ahead and tell me that I'll find in there?"

"Not a thing," I say.

"Okay. I'm going to cuff you, but it's just procedure. You are not under arrest at this time."

"That's fine."

"Hands behind your back, please."

At first, I sit on the hood of his car, making small talk with the other cop who pulls up to act like something's going on. Must be a slow night. Then the cop searching my car walks over with something in his hand. He holds it out between two gloved fingers.

"Do you know what this is?"

My chest sinks into my stomach. I say, "Fuck. What happens now?"

"A rock this size is a felony charge."

"It's not mine, though."

"I have no way of knowing that."

"I understand, but it's not mine. So what steps do I take to get that proven? I've never had a felony."

"You'll go to jail and get a court date, and make your case before the judge. We have to order a test kit to be delivered out here first, but if it is what it looks like—and it is, isn't it?—then you're definitely going to jail tonight. I'm going to escort you into the back of the car now—again, just procedure at this point, until the test kit arrives. You're not under arrest, yet."

It's difficult for every obvious reason to send a text message to the woman you just started dating and liking a whole lot when your wrists are locked behind your back and you're in the backseat of a cop car. Holding the phone at my hip and craning my neck over my shoulder to see the screen, I try to convey what's going on in the least alarming way possible. I get a quick reply back that's just a question mark. I try to explain a little better, the cuffs cutting into my wrists, and the next reply I get is three question marks.

The cop opens the door and I slip the phone into my back pocket.

We walk away from the cars, away from the dashboard cameras, and before they take the cuffs off, the officers of the law explain what's going to happen, and I think of Jermaine saying that before he flashed a gun at me and attempted to steal my drugs.

This is exactly like that. But instead of lighting their arms on fire, I tell the officers, "Thank you."

They take the cuffs off, tell me have a safe night, leave with the meth.

I text Sean, giving him the gist of the shit that just went down, chew him out for leaving drugs in my fucking car. He calls and says I'm tripping. I say, "Sean. He held it all up in my face. It was a big-ass fucking rock, and it wasn't mine."

Sean laughs about it.

I say, "I don't think it's motherfucking funny." I hang up. The next time we talk to each other will be a year and a half from now when he calls from a prison phone and says it'll be thirty years this time on eleven indictments, and he'll laugh then, too, because he's Sean and that's how he'll always be.

It's less than half a mile to Korin's house, less than half a mile to remember how to breathe, to convince myself it'll be okay when she slams the door in my face and never wants to see me again.

My heart beats on the tip of my tongue.

I knock on her door, and she lets me in.

It takes everything in me to keep the tears leveed, to speak with the knot in my throat.

I tell her everything and she listens. Her legs across my lap, her hands locked behind my neck. I want to fall into her eyes and just keep falling, forever. We kiss. She lays my head on her shoulder. We haven't said love yet, but it's what I feel at this moment, going both ways.

WITHDRAWING

I drop a roll of dead presidents on Marshall's table, everything I owe him with my cut included. I only pocket five dollars to compensate driving to his house.

He says, "That's what's up, bro," and holds a fist out and I tap it and he says, "I've got plenty more shit for you."

"Nah," I say, "I'm out."

He flinches, mutes the game show he's watching. "Fuck you talking about?"

"I'm talking about I don't run shit anymore. That, for you, was my last."

"You still tripping over the thing with the cops?" He shoves the air in front of him/curls his lip/shakes his head. "Get out of here with that. Wasn't nothing bad gonna happen."

"I'm not tripping. My head's clearer than it's been in a minute. Look," I pretend to stretch, let my shirt lift enough to show the gun tucked in my waist band, "don't call me no more. I'm out with this shit." I drop my arms and my shirt. "You cool with that?"

He says, "Hey, man, we're good, no worries. You're Sean's brother, man, you do what you do. Nobody's fucking with you."

"Where is Sean?"

"He left for Wharton again this morning. Didn't say when he'd be back. Going back to that crazy bitch that beat up his truck." Marshall shakes his head, smirks. "Your brother's crazy."

"It runs in the family."

Marshall looks at my waist. "Shit, I ain't arguing with that."

We say goodnight and I walk back out to my car and turn the key in the ignition and exhale for what feels like the first time tonight and when I drop the heater in the bushes outside the Sixth Ave convict's house, my hands finally stop shaking.

To every text that asks if I've got some shit, I reply, *I'm done selling*.

This is a quick way to lose friends.

I talk to Vyron at the dealership and he says he's put in for a transfer to Colorado and he'll be leaving in a couple days. He's throwing a party—a fucking rager—and I should come.

I don't, and he moves to Colorado, and I text him *good luck on your new journey,* but I guess he changed his number or something.

I give up the crystal.

The X, too.

I quit everything, and I feel like I might die, but I get by on the feeling of having a life to lose.

I start taking only my prescribed dosage of Adderall.

A gremlin crawls around under my skin. It chews on the nerves in my hands and scratches behind my eyes and thrashes with my spine in its grip.

I bite my nails.

I tell my parents I'm sorry for the grief.

My mom says she loves me, her eyes wet, bottom lip trembling. She says, "If you only knew how hard it was — what you put me through. Nights I spent crying out to god, 'Why? Why can't I help my son?'" A tear rolls down her cheek and she says, "I will always love you. But if you ever start that shit again," she points to the door, says, "There it is."

My dad says, "So you were selling and didn't cut us in on any of it?" Then he wraps his arms around me and squeezes tight and it's a long time before either of us let go.

* * *

I delete half the contact list in my phone. Develop a habit of looking over my shoulder.

I eat more.
   I vomit less.

I take photos out of picture frames and smash the glass covers with a hammer.

On my weekends with the kids, I hug them closer, tighter, longer.

Some days, I smile.
   Some nights, I sleep.

The Union Pacific rattles the walls of my bedroom and I imagine lying on the track, head resting on the rail, and I inhale and hold the breath like it's my last and when I let it out, I feel like I can make it through the day.

I fill notebooks with drawings of mustachioed pigs and wolves on skateboards and cigar-smoking imps.

I turn in a piece of paper that says *I'm out* as my notice of resignation from the entertainment store and I get a job building cabinets.

* * *

I write stories.

I take Korin to places neither of us have ever been before—an upscale Japanese bar, a dinner theater, a two-story Greek-themed coffee house. She never asks where we're going before we get there. She smiles and reaches over the gear shift for my hand and the world is perfect.

I spit bars over Clams Casino and 808 Mafia tracks I download off the internet.

I cradle myself on the floor of the shed and sink my teeth into my knees and scream. Take a minute, remember to breathe. Repeat my new mantra to myself, over and over and over again, until I'm convinced.

Everything is going to be alright.
Everything is going to be alright.
Everything is going to be alright.
Everything is going to be alright.
Everything is going to be alright.
Everything is going to be alright.
Everything is going to be alright.
Everything is going to be alright.
Everything is going to be alright.
Everything is going to be alright.
Everything is going to be alright.
Everything is going to be alright.
Everything is going to be alright.
Everything is going to be

ABOUT THE AUTHOR

Kelby Losack works construction. This is his second novella since his rap career never took off. He lives with his wife in Gulf Coast Texas.

ACKNOWLEDGEMENTS

Fuck-load of thanks to J David Osborne for asking me to write the most difficult and personal thing I hope to ever write. It was a terrible and therapeutic experience and I can't thank you enough for believing in this book.

Of course, all the gratitude in the universe to Mom, Dad, Braden, Sierra, and Cody.

Robert Spencer—there's a line in here that exists on the page because you told me I should use it if I ever write about my experiences with doctors and surgeons. Also, thank you for caring and checking up on me when I was going through that shit.

Justin Carter for reading my works-in-progress and pointing out the shitty parts, back in the day when no one else would give me that honesty and mean well by it.

Gabino Iglesias and Grant Wamack for the steady encouragement and inspiration to put in work.

Rios de la Luz and Troy James Weaver for bearing their souls with zero shame. When I'm scared of being too transparent, I think of both of you and say, "fuck it."

Teresa Pollack and Rick Keeney, your support towards the

indie lit scene is on another level. Thank you, thank you, thank you.

Rob Hart, Bradley Sands, Richard Thomas, and Patrick Wensink for reading my first book before anyone else even knew who I was–that will always mean the world to me.

Jeremy Robert Johnson for being an inspiration and a sweetheart.

To the beautiful voices in the indie lit community: Tiffany Scandal, Michael Kazepis, Cameron Pierce, Matthew Revert, John Wayne Comunale, Scott Adlerberg, Stephen Graham Jones, xTx, Brian Allen Carr, Sam Pink, Andrea Kneeland, Andy de Fonseca, Jennifer Robin, Carlton Mellick III, Rose O'Keefe, John Skipp, Cody Goodfellow, Shane McKenzie, David James Keaton, Nate Southard, Violet LeVoit, Benoit Lelievre, Paul J. Garth, Ed Kurtz, Constance Ann Fitzgerald, Chris Deal, Bud Smith, MP Johnson, Chris Lambert, Christoph Paul, Kevin Maloney, Daniel Vlasaty, Kris Saknussemm, Jeff Burk, Steve Lowe, Jason Wayne Allen, Max Booth III, CV Hunt, David Bowles, Justin Grimbol, Wrath James White... all the other cool people I'm forgetting at the moment.

To the person who bought/stole/was given this copy. Whether you loved or hated it, thank you for your time.

And to Erika, for saving this from being a tragedy, and for encouraging me to stay up all those late nights and write it when I really didn't want to.

Printed in Great Britain
by Amazon